Dares

Dares

Roxanne Morgan

X
LIBRIS

An *X Libris* Book

First published by X Libris in 1995

Copyright © Roxanne Morgan 1995

The moral right of the author has been asserted.

A CIP catalogue for this book
is available from the British Library

ISBN 0 7515 1341 5

Photoset in North Wales by
Derek Doyle & Associates, Mold, Clwyd
Printed and bound in Great Britain by
Clays Ltd, St Ives plc

X Libris
A Division of
Little, Brown and Company (UK)
Brettenham House
Lancaster Place
London WC2E 7EN

Dares

Chapter One

SHANNON GARRETT DROPPED her briefcase into the pannier of the despatch rider's motorcycle. Her folded white linen jacket followed.

The despatch rider stared at her. He moved away from the iron railings at the top of the shop's basement steps, despatch sheet falling to his side.

London's hot summer dust lay in the creases of his leather trousers and biker jacket. He wore heavy boots, and his trousers were padded at thigh and knee. Sweat runnelled down his face. His long fair hair was curly, dusty; and matted with sweat from being under the bike helmet. He was broad across the shoulders. A faint blond stubble covered his cheeks. His eyes were blue. Twenty-five years old, maybe? Twenty-six?

Shannon wordlessly held out the black visored crash helmet that had been resting on his bike. He took it.

'Drive,' she directed. Her voice barely shook.

Shannon swung her leg over the Honda 1000cc motorbike. Her lined linen skirt rucked up to the tops of her thighs, and creased. The leather pillion seat of the bike was hot from standing parked in the summer sun. It moulded itself slightly to her crotch as she sat. She felt the warm leather through her sheer stockings and lace panties.

She leaned forward, her sleeveless shirt-blouse pulling tight over her breasts. To her surprise, her nipples were already hard, painfully erect. I can't believe I'm doing this, she thought.

'Drive,' she repeated, more strongly.

'Look . . . this is a wind-up, yeah? Yeah. You've given your mates sitting over there a laugh.' The man met her gaze. 'If you're *serious*, there's no one in the despatch office, we could go round the back—'

'Just drive,' Shannon said.

The young despatch rider shrugged. He grinned, appreciatively, with a crooked grin. Then he put the crash helmet on. Immediately, black visor down, he became anonymous.

He swung himself on to the bike.

Shannon did not look back. She leaned forward and put her arms around his broad, leather-clad torso.

His body leaned to one side as he kicked the bike into life. The powerful engine roared. The casing of the bike vibrated. Shannon put her feet up on the foot-rests. She spread her legs slightly, and forced her body down. The throbbing vibration of the bike, through the leather seat, pressed against her pussy. She eased forward, pressing the front of her panties down on the seat, bringing her clitoris into contact with the leather.

'Drive!' she said. '*Now.*'

The powerful bike roared out of the side street and into London traffic.

The hot wind of summer caressed her stockinged legs like warm oil. Her hair shook free of its silk-covered elasticated band. She tightened her arms around the man's chest as the bike cornered, feeling hard muscle under the creased leather jacket. She felt his breathing quicken. She leaned back slightly and looked down between their bodies. Old leather trousers, worn soft and pliable, stretched across the rider's buttocks.

The bike heeled over, shot between a bus and a taxi, and, to a blare of horns, sped up Tottenham Court Road. Weaving through the central London lunch-time traffic at sixty miles an hour.

She opened her mouth to speak, but the wind snatched the words from her mouth. She realised, No point in talking. He's got a helmet on. Whatever I do, he can't hear me.

Shannon let go with one hand and brought her arm back. She slid her hand down between their bodies, between the hot leather that stretched across his back, and the thin cotton, already marked with sweat and dust, that clung to her small breasts and flat stomach.

She stroked the taut leather trousers where they stretched across his buttocks.

The bike lurched and recovered.

One hand locked around his body, Shannon caressed the tight, spread buttocks of the rider. The bike shot past a red bus. Shannon, behind black sun-glasses, gazed up at passengers who – for one shocking millisecond – stared down at her.

She removed her hand from the rider's buttocks and slid it up her own thigh.

The bike slowed, caught by traffic lights. She glimpsed a tube station, a major road junction – and people. Hundreds and hundreds of people, in summer suits and dresses, in tourist gear, in T-shirts and tight shorts . . .

Shannon clamped her body against the rider's back. His breathing quickened: she felt his broad chest rise and fall. Her free hand slid secretly up the inside of her stockinged thigh, to her bare cool flesh and suspenders, and then her fingers pushed down inside the front of her lace panties. Warmth met her fingers.

Her pubic hair was soaking. Teasingly, she caressed her little bud, until her inflamed clitoris throbbed.

I can't go through with this . . . can I?

She brought her hand out, and lifted it towards her nostrils.

The lights changed. The bike shot forward.

Shannon whooped, abandoning all caution now. Her legs clamped on to the bike's seat, and again the throbbing of the metal casing aroused her. Behind the anonymous safety of her sunglasses, she laughed at the cars they passed. Streets, trees, lamp-posts, crossing; all gone in a flash, and now they were among high multi-storeyed City buildings.

The despatch rider freed one hand and brought it back behind him. Before Shannon realised, he had grasped her own hand. He pulled her forward. Her sweating body thumped up hard against his muscled back.

He continued to pull her hand forward.

He pressed it down into his crotch.

Shannon closed her hand gently. Worn leather stretched, pushed out by an eight-inch erection. She stroked the length of it. Then, still without entering his clothes, she gripped its girth.

The bike slowed.

Shannon shook her head, frustrated. She hammered with her free hand on his broad back, and then removed her other hand from his throbbing erection. The visored helmet half-turned. Then, the bike began to speed up again. They flashed through canyons between buildings, where towering glass windows glared back in the sun. Seventy m.p.h., seventy-five, eighty . . .

Shannon leaned up against the despatch rider's hot, hard back and slid both her hands around to the front of his body. She stroked his cock through his leather trousers.

His swelling dick hardened, hardened and length-ened. She gripped it tightly and began to move the leather up and down, up and down.

His shoulders stiffened. She felt his arms lock rigid on the handlebars, and the powerful machine swerved coolly between two speeding taxis and shot across three lanes of traffic unscathed. All his muscles tightened; back, shoulders, and powerful thighs gripping the machine.

Shannon moved one hand back. She slid the leather of his pants up and down the shaft of his cock with one hand, and with the other, pressed her fingers into the leather-clad cleft of his buttocks, where his anus should be. His buttocks clamped together, almost trapping her fingers in place. She shifted her hand away from him, pressing her fingers against her spread legs, rubbing her clitoris hard. The bike throbbed in her crotch.

'Ohhh . . .' Shannon slitted her eyes. That they were in London traffic ceased to matter. Fumbling with the fastenings to his trousers, she got one hand down the front. The hot skin of his belly felt slick with sweat. The hard shaft of his cock filled her hand. She ringed it with her thumb and fingers, pulling the foreskin up over his knob. Not able to even see over his shoulder, only able to imagine: is it ivory-coloured, blue-veined, throbbing red, purple . . .?

Shannon thought, in a bewildered haze, *Never like this, it's never been like this!*

The bike sped suddenly free into sunlight, out of City streets and buildings. With iron-willed determin-ation, the rider wrenched the bike across two lanes and began to parallel the Embankment. Tourists in pastel-coloured shirts stood on pavements. One raised a camcorder to film the Tower of London as Shannon and the bike shot past him.

She could not touch the rider's neck or face. The crash helmet covered him. His head turned slightly. She glimpsed nothing but her own face reflected in the black visor, hair streaming, cheeks flushed. He faced forward again.

Her hand plunged deeper into his pants. At the same time she pushed one finger between her own spread legs, down the front of her lace panties, and slid it in and out of her pussy. Her juices covered her hand, and her hot cleft throbbed.

She slid her other hand down the velvet hardness of his dick. The tangled wet hair at his crotch was springy. She scooped his balls into her hand, pressing against the tautness of his pants. His backbone, where she rode pressed against it, arched.

'Now,' she whispered.

She clamped herself to the despatch rider's back. The sun brought smells of leather and man-sweat, sex-juices, and petro-chemicals from the other traffic. She plunged both hands down the front of his pants, one hand kneading his scrotum, the other gripping the shaft of his cock.

She began to bring him off harder, both her hands on his cock. Her legs clamped tight to the motorbike's sides. She pushed her crotch against the pillion seat.

His chest heaved, and she heard him panting, even over the noise of the cars. His back arched, pressing into her breasts. Her nipples strained at her shirt, and her whole breasts ached. She bent her sweating cheek in to his shoulder, smelling leather, clamping her eyes shut.

'Come on, come *on* . . .' Her hand gripped his cock tight. She moved her hand up and down, his hot skin sliding on the shaft. He swelled again in her hand. The blue sky was above them, and girders. Sun flashed off water. The Thames shone below, as they crested the rise and the bike thundered out on to Tower Bridge. She squeezed and slid, squeezed and slid.

The rider's broad body convulsed in her arms. For a second she was standing, feet on the bike's foot-rests, leaning forward, bottom in the air. Her linen skirt remained rucked up to her hips. She felt hot slipstream on her thighs, above her stockings. Hot slipstream that was cold on the soaking crotch of her lace panties.

The rider's back arched.

Hot semen jetted into her hands, inside his leather trousers. He came, rising up from the metal casing of the speeding bike; came again and again into her hands, pelvis thrusting forward, narrow hips jerking in her straining arms, his taut buttocks momentarily thrust up level with her face.

She pressed her whole face into the back of his crotch. She breathed in the smell of sweat, of leather, of semen like flowers and pollen.

The bike's back wheel skidded.

Shannon jolted into the air, made a wild grab at the rider's waist, and sat down with a thump, legs spread wide.

The bike curved around roadworks, ran a red light, and shot off under London Bridge station.

Frustrated, she pushed her crotch against the throbbing seat of the bike. Just the smell of him on her hands made her breathless with wanting. She writhed her body up against him, grinding her breasts into his spine, ignoring the delicious pain.

The despatch bike swung down into side-streets. Narrow roads between warehouses, chain-link fences. The engine's roar echoed off Victorian brick walls.

With a squeal of rubber, the bike halted under a brick arch.

Shannon heard a tinny voice. She realised it was the despatch rider's radio, echoing under this bridge.

Stunned, hands shaking, she sank back and let go of the rider.

'That's—' She panted. 'Not *fair* – you – *I* didn't—'

The bike's rider ignored what she was saying.

Before she could move, he had lifted his leg and dismounted from the bike, propping it on its stand. The last echo of the engine died. The hot side-street, deserted, was utterly silent. A gull cried somewhere over the river.

The rider reached up and jerked the strap of his crash helmet. He swung it off his head, pushing broad hands through his wet fair hair. One hand unzipped his leather jacket. It swung open, disclosing a soft sweat-soaked T-shirt. His muscles shone. The man-smell of sweat and semen breathed off him.

'I—'

Before Shannon could say any more, he stepped behind the bike. She had no time to turn. A broad strong hand slapped her back, between her shoulder-blades, and pushed her body down. Shannon sprawled forward on the bike's metal casing. She threw her arms around the front fork.

She felt his knee on the bike's seat beside her. The bike shook, taking the weight of a second person. His panting breath echoed under the bridge.

Shannon found herself sprawled forward, breasts pushed into the hot metal of the bike casing. Her shirt was jerked firmly up. One hand kept her pressed down, his other hand, underneath her, gripped her breasts, kneading them until she bit her lip, and then threw her head back and up. 'Ahhh . . .'

Her feet were still on the rests, pushing her bottom up into the air, higher than her head now.

His hand jerked free, and tugged her skirt up over her buttocks, around her waist.

His fingers hooked under the back of her lace

panties and yanked them down.

Summer air swept cool across her naked buttocks and pussy. His hands gripped and caressed her stocking-covered legs, then slid upwards and away.

Behind her, she heard the sound of a zip pulled down.

Unbelievably, she felt herself arch her body down, pushing her buttocks higher.

He straddled her and the bike together.

His muscled thighs pushed against the back of her thighs, his skin hot and running with sweat. Fingers briefly caressed her buttocks. His newly-erect cock slapped against her pussy.

She felt him bring a hand up and guide it in. The thickness of the head of his cock pushed her apart, her soaking juices sliding him in. She pushed her body up and back, against his cock and balls and belly. His shaft slid deep into her vagina. She gripped him, hot and clenching and craving. His strong hands grabbed her hips and pulled her to him as he thrust.

Her whole body arched up.

More than ready, shivering with pleasure delayed, she came in a searing burst of pleasure; came again and again, sweating bare stomach pressed against the leather of the bike seat, arms gripping the hard metal, his firm hands grabbing her waist, his thick sex impaling her, her pussy clenching again and again on his cock, until he came for the second time, and they sprawled together, panting, breathing echoing under the brickwork of Southwark Bridge.

At last, his voice his beside her ear, panting, said, 'I don't even know your name!'

Shannon pushed herself upright. She began to clean and straighten her clothes with shaking fingers, and stuttered something, she herself didn't know what.

His hot semen slid from deep in her pussy and

slicked the seat of the motorbike.

Feeling that, a great relaxation and satisfaction swept through her. She smiled and turned her face towards the sun. 'It's been lovely, thank you. Goodbye.'

' "Goodbye"?' he protested plaintively. 'But won't I see you again, darlin'?'

'No,' Shannon said simply.

His blue eyes were very puzzled. 'I don't get it, doll. Why not?'

'Because I don't want to,' Shannon said. 'That isn't why I did it. Oh – there is something you can give me, though. No, not money. *That*.'

She reached over and tore the first despatch sheet off his pad. His voice echoed down the back-streets towards London Bridge Station. 'But *why . . .?*'

Shannon smiled reflectively, casting her mind back towards lunch-time.

. . . Shannon Garrett was late for lunch.

The sun beat down into the narrow London streets. Her heeled sandals kicked up dust as she took the short cut through St Giles churchyard and emerged, sweating, below Denmark Street.

She took a moment to check her reflection in a shop window. White blouse and cream skirt, and a white linen jacket; briefcase in hand . . . she peered closer, seeing a woman who did not quite look to be thirty, with curly hair pulled back at the sides – brown hair, but the shop window glass turned it almost auburn.

You could not tell, Shannon decided, that she had been crying. Her eyes were not puffy, or smudged.

Across the road, someone waved.

Shannon picked out Nadia Kay immediately from the throng sitting at the tables outside the Café Valletta. The red-haired woman lifted her hand again, waved languidly, and smiled. Sunglasses hid her eyes. Shannon waved back and crossed the busy road.

'You managed to leave the shop, then?' Shannon sat down beside Nadia, in the meagre shade of a lime tree.

'My father's looking after it for a couple of hours. He's such an old dear.' Nadia removed her sunglasses, briefly displaying eyes with sweepingly long, dark red lashes. A few faint crow's feet hinted that she was a decade older than Shannon. A trickle of sweat ran down her freckled shoulders, across her collarbone, vanished down the neck of her ecru linen dress. 'Shannon, is something the matter?'

'No,' Shannon said unconvincingly.

The scent of human sweat was in the air from the young men and women crowded into the Café Valletta. Not unpleasant. Warm bodies, sleeves rolled up, necklines low. A loud hum of talk. The lunch-time business drinkers: City types, arty types. Shannon took a guilty look round in case any of the other staff from *Femme* magazine should be here. No, no one.

'Corey's getting drinks from the bar,' Nadia remarked, leaning back to look into the crowd inside the café. The sun had already brought a slight flush to her bare, cream-skinned arms. 'I told her to get one for you. What's upset you?'

'It's . . .' Shannon's face crumpled. She sat down next to Nadia in a white plastic chair. 'I've broken up with Tim. I have *finally* done it. I'm glad I've done it!'

Nadia stubbed out a slim cigarette. 'He was never going to leave Julia. I'm glad you realised.'

'Oh, I always knew. It's just that, when I told him, he cried. He cried, Nadia, like always; and he said that he would leave her, it was just the kids, but he would do it, give him time.'

'And you said?'

Shannon took a deep breath. 'I surprised myself. I

said, *I've heard that shit too many times before. Get out.*
And – and he *went*. After six years!'

'I shall find you a man,' Nadia announced, when
Shannon had stopped crying. 'There's nothing like a
new lover to restore your confidence – so long as you
don't fall in love with him.'

A new voice said, 'He'll only turn into a wimp,
whoever he is.'

A tall girl with short black hair stood over the table,
carrying three glasses with care. As she put them
down, and smoothed her wet palms down her black
summer dress, she smiled at Shannon.

'Only two kinds of men. Wimps and bastards,'
Corey Black said.

Shannon dabbed at her eyes. 'I always forget you've
been divorced. You seem so young.'

'Married at eighteen, divorced at twenty,' the girl
said.

'Tim was a wimp. I always knew that. Except, in
bed . . .' Shannon looked at her two friends. 'Wouldn't
it be good if we could just have sex with the men we
want, without bothering about the rest of it?'

Red-haired Nadia smiled enigmatically. 'Good in
theory, but you wouldn't do it, my dear.'

'I would, too,' Shannon growled. 'I know what you
think about me. Boring old Shannon, works in an
office, with a married boyfriend – what a mouse!'

'My dear, we don't!'

Somewhat mollified by the genuine concern in
Nadia's voice, Shannon finished, 'I'd do anything you
two would do!'

Corey pointed across the road to the corner of
Denmark Street. 'Well, I bet you wouldn't pick *him* up.
Not a chat-up. Just a fuck. Go on, I dare you.'

Nadia joined in with the young girl's laughter. 'Yes.
We dare you!'

12

Shannon was silent for a minute.

She looked across the road, at the despatch rider.

'If I take the dare,' she said slowly, 'if I bring you proof, then – what do I win?'

Nadia smiled. 'Why . . . you get to dare both of *us*. That seems fair. Don't you think so, Corey?'

'Sure,' Corey said. 'Why not? But I know Shannon! She'll never do it.'

Shannon stood up . . .

Shannon Garrett walked up from the Tottenham Court Road Underground station to the Café Valletta, jacket over her arm, briefcase swinging from one hand. She smiled gently. Sometimes she hummed under her breath.

The lunch-time clientele had left the café-bar two hours ago. It was not yet time for the evening drinkers. Nadia Kay and Corey Black still sat together, lazily, at the table under the lime tree.

'Hey, Shannon!' The younger woman waved.

Nadia silently lifted her glass.

Shannon pulled up one of the white chairs and put her briefcase and jacket carefully on it. Then she threw a piece of paper down on the table, among the empty glasses and Nadia's gold-banded cigarette stubs.

'Proof,' Shannon said.

Corey leaned forward and looked.

A despatch rider's sheet, with signatures as far as 1 p.m. After that, nothing but two scrawled kisses.

The black-haired girl leaned back, a vaguely discontented expression on her face. 'We know you went off with him. We saw. That isn't proof that you *did* anything with him.'

Nadia interrupted. 'Don't be naive, my dear. You only have to look at her.'

'Yes, but—' Corey looked up. Shannon saw her take

in the creased skirt and blouse, and what Shannon felt must surely be her burning, flushed face.

Corey suddenly grinned. 'Oh, wow! Shannon, you're going to tell us all about it, aren't you?'

'Maybe.' Shannon called the waiter over and ordered Pimm's and lemonade. She eased herself into another of the white chairs. She reached over and pulled her briefcase on to her lap, and took out two folded pieces of paper. 'But before I do . . . this *was* a dare. Remember what we agreed. I did my part of it – now *I* dare both of you.'

Shannon smiled.

'While I was coming back here on the Tube, I had time to be inventive.'

She held up two folded papers.

'Take one,' she invited. 'Go on. I dare you.'

'Oh, you can't seriously . . .' Corey's voice trailed off. Suddenly bright red, she buried her nose in her own glass of Pimm's and drank deeply. She mumbled, 'It was just a joke. Surely.'

Nadia smiled. When she took off her sunglasses, Shannon saw that the older woman's eyes were bright with amusement, and something more like excitement than her usual pose of ennui. 'Corey, sweets, we *did* agree . . .'

Shannon, her body still tingling, grinned at the girl.

Corey's eyes flashed. 'I can take a dare! No one can say I can't!' She snatched one of the folded pieces of paper out of Shannon's hand.

'Fair's fair,' Nadia agreed. She took the other.

Chapter Two

NADIA KAY PAUSED with her key in the lock of *Ephemera*. One hand was poised to turn the notice beside the shop door from CLOSED to OPEN. She hesitated, staring out from behind her shop window into the Neal's Yard arcade.

Nine-thirty in the morning. A few early tourists.

Irresolute, she turned back into the tiny shop. Brooches, cups, mirrors, rings, carved wooden crocodiles, Victorian bird-cages, beads, bells, hand-made pots, Russian icons – all glittering, brightly-coloured, designed to lure in the wealthy tourist. The shop smelled of amber incense.

She slapped the key down on the mahogany counter top, picked up the phone, and dialled.

A voice answered, 'Features editor, *Femme*, can I help you?'

'It's Nadia,' she said.

'Oh, Nadia, hello. It's okay, there's no one in the office at the moment.' Shannon Garrett's voice still had what Nadia thought to be an uncharacteristic purr in it. 'I was going to call you. I keep thinking – did it happen? It did happen! I can't believe it happened!'

Nadia waited until the younger woman had stopped

bubbling at her.

'I wanted to ask you.' Nadia paused. A not particularly well-dressed man wandered past the shop window, studied two netsuke in the glass cabinet, and continued on. 'Shannon . . . I can't possibly do this!'

'Why not?'

'You make it sound so reasonable! Oh, my dear, a lover is one thing – you know Oscar had his little friends, and he never objected to me having mine. Encouraged it, if anything. But I expected to know their social circle, I expected them to take me out to dinner at least, to entertain me—'

'Did they?'

A pause. 'What?'

'Did they *entertain* you? Nadia, I think that's why I stayed with Tim so long. I'd got tired of being bored from starter through to dessert! That was what was so wonderful about yesterday. I didn't have to ask how he liked his coffee. I didn't have to ask his name. I'm tired of hearing how bad it is at the office, and how his mother preferred his younger brother to him, and how his school life was a misery. I just wanted his body, Nadia, and I had it, and I didn't even have to tell him he was wonderful!'

Nadia chewed her lip.

'Besides,' the voice on the phone protested, 'it was a dare. How long have we known each other, Nadia?'

'Ten years,' she answered automatically.

'And we've both known Corey since she was a young teenager. We've always kept our promises to each other.'

Nadia drummed her fingers on the shop counter.

Shannon's voice on the phone was mischievous. 'Beside, if you back out of a dare, that's probably a double penalty. I quite surprised myself on the train coming back, with what I could think up. By the way, which one did you get? Nadia? Hello?'

'I've just had an idea,' Nadia said. 'Oh, you'll know which one I got when I bring the proof. Lunch on Tuesday, as usual.'

She gently replaced the phone on its cradle.

'Curious, but exciting,' Nadia Kay decided softly, 'hunting young men at my age.'

No one heard her speak. She cruised down the deserted Embankment in her red MG sports car. Unseasonable June rain fell, misting the afternoon and the rustling plane trees. A boat on the river sounded a siren. Her emerald green light raincoat fell back from her sheer-stockinged legs as she shifted down the gears.

The teenage boy was walking down the pavement ahead of her.

He has such clear skin! Nadia thought, amazed. And he's so thin!

No more than fourteen, fifteen. The boy hesitated. He stopped, squatted, and began to re-tie the laces on one of his worn combat boots. Rain drops shone in his red hair. It was caught back from his eyes by a black bandanna. Spots of water darkened the ripped sleeveless black T-shirt stretched across his broad back. His shoulders were wide and freckled. His T-shirt rode up out of the back of his tattered black jeans. Nadia saw pale flesh in the gap.

His eyes flicked up as she slowly cruised the pavement.

His gaze lingered appreciatively on the gleaming red polish of the MG, caressed the classic curving lines of its wing, moved up to the driver – and his gaze became utterly blank.

He gave his boot a last tug, stood up, and loped away down the Embankment.

Nadia swore.

Three separate cars and a taxi blared horns as she swung the MG across the road, crossed the opposite lane, shot up a side-street, and screeched to a halt with two wheels up on the low pavement, outside a grey concrete and glass building.

She stared up the concrete stairs to the entrance, not seeing what she was looking at for fury. Closed glass doors, now streaked with rain. Beyond them, greyboard-lined walls with dog-eared University notices pinned up on them. Young men and women swarmed aimlessly inside the reception area.

Damn him, he didn't even see *me!* He has no right!

The sky darkened above the soot-stained London college. Young men in ragged jeans or combat trousers, and T-shirts with logos, walked inside with rare self-possession. No one looked out through the doors at her. Even the male receptionist ignored her.

'Perhaps I look like someone's mother,' she muttered viciously.

Nadia hit the wheel of her MG with her fist.

Anything over twenty-two doesn't exist, is that it? Bloody hell!

The rain fell harder now. Urban summer rain: it brought with it a strong smell through her half-open car window of road-tar, green plane leaves, and petrol. A boy stepped under the protection of the college entrance. Rain spotted his white t-shirt. He stood with his thumbs tucked under the heavy leather belt of his faded jeans.

She recognised the general area of Temple Underground station. This was one of the side-streets leading up to the Strand. The building had a college name over the door which she vaguely knew.

She took Shannon's scribbled note from the pocket of her light raincoat. It was direct and to the point.

I dare you to seduce a young male virgin.

As to that, she thought, now I'm in completely the wrong place! These young men here are eighteen, nineteen, twenty. Anything I'd be attracted to has no doubt long since ceased to be a virgin. Damn that Shannon!

The young men and women swarmed out of the doors. Idly, she noted the boy still waiting under the shelter of the entrance. Too young to be a student, surely?

The rain briefly eased.

The boy moved to the bottom step and looked back at her. Then he looked away. Then back.

He was fair-haired, with hulking shoulders for so young a man, wearing blue jeans with a wide belt, and a white T-shirt, and no jacket. His arms were bare to the rain.

Nadia clapped her battered green silk trilby on to her short red hair, and paused to glance in the rear-view mirror and coax a wisp of a curl out from behind her gold-studded ear. The natural deep red of her hair made her skin appear to glow in the soft afternoon.

The boy came up to her as she locked the car door from the outside.

She looked up from under long lashes.

'Good car,' he said. 'I was just noticing it was a good car. I mean. Sorry. I wasn't staring at you, honest.'

Up close he had long, strongly-muscled legs, and a stomach flat as a washboard. His fair hair flopped over his face, and he stooped, unconsciously, being several inches taller than Nadia. She let her gaze sweep from his Doc Martin boots, up the faded blue denim of his jeans, and linger momentarily at his crotch. A small bulge hinted at a hard-on.

'Are you one of the students here?' she asked.

'Yes – no – if I get my grades, I will be, in October

19

next year. My brother's here already.'

No more than sixteen, then. He made as if to move away, up to the glass doors. He stopped. Nadia watched a dark red flush creep up from the white neck of his T-shirt, up his throat, and darken his face up to his blond hairline.

'Part of this building is older, isn't it?' she said. 'I remember a friend of mine recommended it as having one of the finest small eighteenth-century chapels still extant. Is that so?'

'I know where it is. I could show you. They gave us a tour this morning, for next year's students.' His blush had not faded. 'Please, let me show you. This way's easiest.'

He ducked his head and loped up the side-street, in the rain, turning towards the Strand. Nadia followed, heels tapping on the wet pavement. Every so often the boy looked anxiously back to make sure that she followed. She watched his tight buttocks move under the blue denim.

At the Strand entrance, it was obvious that the building had been impressive once. Nadia entered the wide foyer, noting red-carpeted marble stairs to the upper floors, a high moulded plaster ceiling.

'It's up here, uh, miss, uh.'

'My name is Nadia.' She smiled, letting him precede her up the shabbily carpeted stairs. There were fewer other students here. Two Asian girls passed her, walking down.

There was a tall door ahead. He opened it and entered the chapel. She followed him.

It was dark, even at midday. Dark, and a little cold. She reached up and brushed the wet red hair out of her eyes. Wooden pews stretched out in front of her, down towards the altar, and candy-twist pillars lined the aisle.

His husky, deep young voice behind her said, 'I could wait, if you want. I could show you back out when you've finished.'

Nadia rested one hand on the back of a pew. She unbuttoned her raincoat, letting it swing open over the Chinese-style olive-green silk dress that she wore.

'An interesting late example of a box-pew,' she murmured, turning and stepping past him. She steadied herself with one hand on his bare arm.

The boy's fair skin flushed again. He scowled, half-smiled, standing with his hands dangling at his sides, his eyes fixed on her. There was definitely a bulge in his jeans now, Nadia saw, bulking out the faded fly. She blinked at the sheer size of it.

'Stained-glass windows,' he muttered. Clumsily, he pointed up at the blue and red glass, and brushed his arm against her silk-clad shoulder as he brought it down.

'Oh, yes. How beautiful.' Nadia smiled, apparently oblivious.

'I think,' she said, after the appallingly tedious fifteen minutes she felt obliged to spend studying the chapel and its hideous green- and yellow-painted walls, 'I do think that we should go and have tea somewhere. It's the least I can do, since you've been so helpful – what do you say to Fortnum and Mason?'

The red MG had a parking ticket when they came out. She chuckled and threw it on to the back seat.

He brushed her spine, between her shoulder-blades, helping her into her car. After that she drove rapidly and skilfully through London traffic to Piccadilly in the rain, and, in the windscreen, watched his reflection. His bare arms were spotted with rain, the fair hairs erect. Defined biceps – yes, he lifts weights, she thought. I recognise it from my friends' sons.

Fortnum and Masons, crowded, had its usual perfect

smell of spices and coffee. Nadia took the boy to her favourite table, towards the back, and ordered black coffee and cream gateaux.

'It's very good of you,' the boy said. His accent was good, she noticed, and he seemed well-mannered, if somewhat out of his depth. She grinned to herself.

I very much doubt this is within the terms of Shannon's dare. But what the hell, it doesn't happen every day . . .

Nadia dipped the end of her index finger into her cream cake, and licked at it delicately. 'Pure self-indulgence, don't you think?'

The young man's eyes were fixed on her, pupils wide and dark. She put her cream-covered finger into her mouth and sucked it. Then she held up her finger and ran her tongue up it from root to tip.

'Uh,' he said.

After the end of the tea, she led him out the back way, into the street where the MG was parked.

'You've been so very helpful.' Faint rain misted her skin. 'I would like to give you another reward. If you can think of one.'

He swallowed; she saw his throat move. His brilliant blue eyes fixed on her. With a voice that dropped into huskiness, he said, 'I want to kiss you.'

She put her hands flat against his chest. The cotton of his T-shirt was warm from his body. She felt his pulse under her hands.

'Yes,' she said simply, lifting her mouth.

His lips were soft, and the smell of them suddenly loosened her body. She moved against him, lifting her hands and grabbing his head, and bringing his mouth down. His warm breath feathered her cheek, then his lips fastened hard on hers, and his hot tongue flicked out to touch hers.

The effect was electric. All her senses heightened:

22

she became conscious of the rain on her face, the silk on her skin, and the huge and warm breathing body of the boy-man pressed against her. Strong arms encircled her, uncertain, as if he thought she might break.

'Oh God, you're beautiful.' His voice cracked.

The bulge in his jeans was enormous. She pressed her body urgently against it.

'I know – a hotel—' Her breathing was rapid. Her head whirled. The hotel was a rendezvous she had often made use of when married to Oscar. She had no memory this time of walking to the small, select street; of making the booking. All she was conscious of was the strong young body next to her, and how he kept stealing glances at her, his eyes darkening with desire.

At last she closed the hotel room door behind her.

'This isn't . . .' She slid her hands up under his T-shirt, startled at the heat of his smooth skin. 'This isn't your first time.'

'That was just *girls*.' He shivered like a horse. She ran a cupped hand soothingly round his beardless cheek.

Nadia slowly unbuttoned the top buttons of her silk dress. Without looking down, she slid one hand down the front of his body, over his belt-buckle, and down the fly of his jeans. She cupped his bulging crotch. His thick cock was hot and hard through the soft material.

His hips thrust forward. Suddenly he grabbed her shoulders, pulling her coat down so that it trapped her arms at her sides, and shoved his face into her breasts.

'You don't – have to hurry—' Nadia staggered back, off-balance. She tried to reach out, but couldn't. The soft counterpaned bed caught her behind the knee.

She sprawled on the bed. One heeled shoe went, knocked flying across the room. The boy fell on top of her. His solid body covered her from her feet to her shoulders, blond hair brushing her lips as he gnawed frantically at her breasts.

'Wait—' One of her breasts was squeezed out of her silk dress. The boy's head darted down. His tongue licked her nipple, hard as a little stone, and then his mouth fastened on her, sucking and biting.

She arched her back, trying to push her bare breast further into his mouth. Both her arms were pinioned. She pulled one leg up, stroking his denim-clad leg with her calf, and then lifted her foot until she could tuck the heel into the cleft of his buttocks. She pulled his body sharply towards her and down, feeling the bulge in his jeans push into her crotch, sliding on her silky knickers.

His startled voice cried, '*Shit!*'

Her body was suddenly free of weight. Nadia's head jerked up.

She lifted herself up on her elbows on the bed.

The boy knelt up between her legs, looking down at himself. His face was scarlet. A wet patch was spreading on the crotch of his jeans even as Nadia looked.

'Oh *no*,' he groaned.

'That,' Nadia said, with a wicked smile, 'is nothing to worry about. It often happens with young men. Fortunately it's easily cured.'

She half sat up, slid her arms out of the sleeves of the raincoat, and lay back again. Slowly and deliberately, she unbuttoned her Chinese silk dress.

'Oh God,' he said, 'I want you!'

Her sheer stockings were held up by a lacy white suspender belt. She wore a lacy white bra, and a tiny pair of white satin knickers. Nadia slid her hands down her body. Over her small, firm breasts, gently curved tummy and slim hips. And then, smoothing the satin behind her, cupping her trim buttocks.

The boy sat down cautiously on the bed. She touched his arm. His skin was white, soft, and the muscle underneath rock-solid. She kneaded it gently. 'I want to watch you undress.'

'You want to watch *me?*' A grin tugged one corner of his mouth.

In one movement he put his arms back over his shoulders and stripped his T-shirt forward and off. Nadia watched the light from the hotel windows fall like water on his solid, bulky shoulders and the defined pectorals of his torso. A thin feather of dark blond hair crept up from the waistband of his blue jeans. She slid her hand from his throat to his navel. His skin was utterly smooth and unmarked.

A tension stiffened his shoulders. More awkward now, he stood. His hands went to his flies again, unbuttoning them slowly, silver button after silver button. Then he took his hands away and slid his jeans and boxer shorts together down his hips, down his thighs, and ended in an undignified tangle, standing on one leg.

'You could have taken your boots off first,' Nadia pointed out demurely. His eyes flashed at her from under dark-blond brows. Then he grinned again. His half-flaccid organ bobbed between his legs as he unlaced his boots.

He's so *big!* Nadia thought. Good grief. How wonderful.

The boots thumped on to the carpet.

He stood, naked. She looked up at him from the bed, the sharply-defined triangular shape of his broad shoulders and narrow hips. Smooth-skinned thighs, heavily muscled, and a rough dark bush of hair at the fork of his body from which his cock sprang, newly erect, with a purple engorged head.

'Politeness has no place in bed,' Nadia said. 'I want

your big, beautiful cock inside me. *Fuck me!'*

She barely got the words out. He tumbled her back on to the sheets, pressing her shoulders down on the pillow, pushing her legs apart with his knees. Then, hesitantly, he lowered himself down. The hot, velvety warmth of his skin pressed against her breasts, her stomach, and between her thighs. She clasped her legs around him, pushing her pubic mound up against his stiff rod.

'I want you!' He bent down and kissed her savagely and inexpertly, his weight almost crushing her.

She slid her arms down his smooth flanks, pressing her palms into his warm skin. Suddenly she clutched at his tight buttocks, pressing him to her. He bit at her collar-bone, gnawing and nipping, and, as she breathlessly gasped, worried at her like a dog, biting down the tender skin over her ribs and across her stomach.

'Woman!' His voice was deep, resonant, breaking at the last on a cracked note.

She rolled over, rising above him. To see him sprawled back on the bed, naked, made her pussy throb. His cock rose taut out of the bush of brown hair at his groin.

She leaned forward and began to lick at the side of the shaft. She heard him moan. Ignoring him, ignoring how hard his reaching hands closed on her breasts, she nibbled at his balls, burying her face in his hot, damp hair. Then she lifted her head, and stroked his cock from root to tip with a slow tongue.

'Oh, Jesus!' he yelled.

She took his thick cock into her mouth and sucked, rubbing her lips up and down the shaft, up and down, until he swelled, and his hips arched under her, and she threw her arms around his buttocks and sucked him until he came.

26

He lay spent for no more than seconds. 'Oh my God,' she said softly; and got no more words out. His mouth came down on hers. She reached between their bodies, marvelling at his flat muscular stomach. The wisp of stomach-hair tangled in her fingers, and she followed it down to his crotch, caressing his swollen, taut balls. She grasped the shaft of his cock. It swelled again instantly in her hand. She began to tease her pussy with the head of it, brushing the tip against the outer walls of her labia. Her sex swelled, opened, dampened.

'Ahh!' He pushed inside her, pushed deep. She took him, her hips rising, her back arching, feeling him thick inside her, feeling the head of his cock rubbing at the narrowest part of her sex, teasing and exciting, until she wrapped her legs around his waist and rhythmically pulled him deep, deep inside. His young hard body thumped against her spread inner thighs, her crotch, her pussy. Mercilessly she squeezed down on him, until his cock slid in her juices, and his balls banged against her anus. Her sex convulsed. Pleasure lifted her hips, lifted her body, blazed through her; flushing her pale skin pink, loosening every muscle, searing into her.

With a triumphant shout she rolled over, him in her arms, until she came to a rest half on, half off the bed.

He curled against her back as his cock shrank and slipped from her. They lay for a long time, together. He touched her body wonderingly, from her slender feet to her soft thighs, from her arms to her breasts, all the time his face alight.

The clock on the hotel mantelpiece chimed four.

'I won't see you again, will I?' the boy said wistfully.

'No. It would spoil it.'

'I just wish I had something I could give you. A gift.' He looked around. 'I don't have anything to give.'

27

Nadia paused, where she sat on the edge of the bed, half dressed, in white bra, knickers, stockings and trilby hat. She remembered Shannon's scrawled note in her raincoat pocket.

'No gifts. No proof,' she said. She reached across to him, sliding her hands into his half done up denim jeans. His cock was already stiffening.

'I really *do* have to go now,' she breathed. 'I do. I – oh!'

Shannon Garrett sat in the Café Valletta at midday on the Tuesday. It was raining again. The water ran down the windows, streaking the plate glass between the big potted ferns. Resounding chatter from the bar made the Café Valletta sound like a hothouse aviary.

She studied Nadia's piece of paper, on the table. A paper smearily duplicated, with a scrawled signature, and contained in a transparent plastic case.

'A *parking ticket?*' she exclaimed. 'What kind of proof is that?'

'Two parking tickets.' Nadia Kay smiled dreamily. 'You'll believe me when I tell you.'

'Well . . .' Shannon muttered, not convinced.

Corey's voice interrupted. 'That's *my* proof,' she said, throwing a fat envelope down on the table.

Shannon undid the flap. She looked inside. With one finger she paged carefully through the contents. Then she looked up, amazed.

'Corey, there must be five thousand pounds here!'

Corey Black looked smug.

'What happened?' Shannon demanded.

The younger woman took off her leather jacket and slung it over the back of her chair. A waiter took her order for coffee. She sat down.

'OK,' she said at last. 'It was the day after we had lunch last week. I had a shoot with Perry. Last Wednesday . . .'

Chapter Three

'OK, *GIVE THAT* smile! Now turn. Hold it. That face! Those eyes, give me *those eyes*. Head left a little . . . that's it . . . smile! Turn again, other side . . . oh, you're beautiful, yes you are . . .'

The catalogue photographer kept a constant flow of instructions in the air. Corey Black whirled on the spot, smiling, with her back to a white wall, and the umbrella-backed lights in her eyes.

'OK, take five. That's wonderful, sweetheart. Keeps 'em happy at *Homestead*.'

'Uh-huh.' Corey stretched her arms, relieving muscle tension. She grinned, then, and did a perfect glide down past the lights into the little W14 back room. 'Four inches taller and I could have been a cat-walk model. Story of my life.'

'Mail order catalogues pay the rent,' the photographer, Perry, remarked.

Corey shrugged. 'I'm getting enough work as a photographer myself. Modelling is just jam. Portraits, mostly. I *hate* kid's photo-portraits, but they pay . . . what are you using there?'

Ten minutes' discussion about different makes of camera and speeds of film ate up the coffee break. It wasn't until she had changed into another outfit, and done another sheet of contacts, that she got a chance to speak to Serena.

'Serena . . .' She checked that Perry was deep in consideration of his film stock. 'Want to ask you something.'

'Of course, sweetie.' Serena smiled. She had a sharp exterior that concealed a surprisingly air-headed character, Corey thought. She was elegant, if you had to give her a word, and far, *far* too well-dressed to be a professional photographer's assistant, even as a butterfly-minded hobby.

'What is it?' Serena asked.

'I've got a dare on,' Corey said bluntly. 'With a friend of mine. She dared me to do it for money. I want to do it for so *much* money that it's going to shock her little cotton socks off.'

' "It"?' Serena murmured, her eyes on Perry's back.

'Fuck,' Corey said. 'You know. Sleep with. Leg-over job. Have it off with someone. F-U—'

Serena chuckled. 'No lack of opportunity, sweetie. These days, nice girls do.'

Nice Sloane girls with private school diplomas and long legs, Corey marvelled. Beats me why. But then, I don't move in those circles.

'Is this a career change,' the leggy blonde enquired delicately, 'or a one-off?'

'One-off.'

'Mmm . . . how soon do you want to do this?'

Lunch is on Tuesday, Corey thought. 'How about this weekend?'

'Well, I don't know, sweetie. It's short notice. Tell you what. Leave your answerphone on. I'll see if anyone's giving out invitations.'

Two days later, on the Friday, Corey returned to her flat and played back that day's answerphone messages.

'Corey, darling! I've got a man you simply must meet. He's only going to be in town for a few days. Come to Quaglino's for dinner on Saturday. I may not be able to stay long myself, but I'll introduce you to him. Oh, and don't think I'm being rude, but I can lend you one of my frocks to wear.' Beeep!

Corey Black paused at the top of the white marble steps going down into Quaglino's main dining area.

She wore her favourite lace-up combat boots and torn black leggings. Over the leggings, she had put a long ragged skirt composed of layer upon layer of heavy black lace. This was belted with a wide black leather strap. Its chunky buckle read BITCH. Above that, she wore her favourite black bustier, and her studded, high-cut leather jacket.

She wore no jewellery, except for the heavy skull pendant around her throat. She had spiked her black hair in a soft fall, and smudged Goth black eyeshadow in the sockets of her eyes.

She extended one hand. She wore silver-studded, fingerless leather gloves. She rested her hand on the rail that was composed of golden metal interlocked Qs and looked down across the tables for Serena. The noise level at the densely packed hundred tables dropped.

'Corey!' a voice hissed. 'Oh, sweetie!'

Corey waved and walked down the fourteen marble steps. The chatter of the diners began again. Serena swept to the foot of the steps, between dinner-goers and frantic but organised staff. She glared up. She was wearing an elegant pink suit. 'Just what do you think you're doing?' she snapped.

'*I* like it,' Corey said. 'Well, where is he, then?'

'Coming in here like this, showing me up – I am never speaking to you again, Corey Black!' Serena

31

turned on her high heel and strode elegantly towards a table towards the rear. Corey followed her through the crowds.

I'm not nervous, she thought as she sat down, and then realised that she was being ordered better food and wine than she could appreciate for nerves, by a man she dared not look at. She sneaked a glance. Broad-shouldered in an elegant dark suit, with heavy silver cuff-links: a white-haired American who looked to be in his sixties.

Oh, *what!* she thought.

'Corey and I are just going to the washroom,' Serena trilled. '*Aren't we, sweetie.*'

'He's old! He's American!' Corey protested, in the taupe-plush and mirror-filled Ladies' room. 'I thought you were going to find me an Arab prince or something.'

'You haven't studied *Investor's Chronicle*.' Serena coolly reapplied her lipstick. Her eyes wouldn't meet Corey's in the mirror. 'Sweets, a really rich man wouldn't take the chance of being turned down after a one-off . . . His name is William Caryll Jenson. He comes from California. His companies invested early in aerospace information technology. He's rich enough for you. I'd say you could go home with four hundred pounds.'

Corey blinked. 'Do you, ah, that is—'

'Sweetie, I wouldn't get into bed for four hundred pounds. I must go. Ronnie phoned. He wants me to fly out to Bahrain with him tonight – rush invitation.' She patted her crocodile bag. 'Passport. Must run. Give my love to William.'

'Yeah,' Corey muttered gloomily after the blonde left the Ladies', 'I'll tell him "the snotty bitch says goodbye".'

I could just walk out of here. I don't even have to go

back to the table. Shannon can stuff her dare.

It's a real shame. He looks kind of nice.

Corey was still irresolute when she left the Ladies'. She realized then that she had left her leather jacket hooked over the back of her chair (worth it if only for Serena's appalled expression) and would therefore have to go back and get it.

She walked back between the crowded tables. The American sat alone at their table, one arm stretched out along the back of another chair. He *occupied* the space around him, Corey thought, trying to put a word to a feeling. Sheppard and Anderson suit, silk tie, the manicured air of wealth – and yet, that craggy face and silver hair ... For the first time she met his gaze for more than a split second. 'The snotty bitch says goodbye.'

He had a full head of silver hair that spilled unruly curls over his lined brow. More lines creased at the corners of his eyes as he laughed resonantly. He leaned forward and took her hand. 'You're something new, miss, I'll give you that.'

I have to do this, Corey thought. Unconsciously she shifted in her seat. Her mouth felt dry. Mixed in with the apprehension was a curious excitement.

She picked up her fork and prodded warningly at her *fruits de mer*. 'And I'm not going to sit here and listen to you talk about the Californian aerospace industry *either*. I've got enough friends in engineering already who can bore me rigid.'

He had bright eyes deeply set under hairy brows, and they twinkled when he said, 'What shall we talk about, then?'

He didn't look right in a suit. He was the kind of businessman who would take full weekends off to go rock-climbing and leave behind men half his age, she thought. Or back-packing, or hunting. Something outdoors and physical.

'There *is* something I always wanted to ask.' Corey took another look around at the raucous, well-dressed diners. 'What's it like to be rich?'

'Come and see,' he said.

He did not drive himself, naturally. Corey followed him into the back of the stretch limo. She felt herself choose, standing there on the London pavement with the hot dusk turning to night. She got into the car.

The excitement buzzing in her head made her hardly conscious of the drive, the entrance to his apartment building, the penthouse lift. She wandered open-mouthed through the sumptuous rooms.

'Here,' he said.

Corey pressed the remote he handed her. The floor-length drapes slid aside. She exclaimed, 'Yes!'

The apartment's bedroom window extended from floor to ceiling, from wall to wall. She approached it cautiously. The lights of London shone twenty-six floors below. She edged closer to the point where carpet and glass met, leaning to look down.

'Bought this little place for my second wife,' William Jenson rumbled. 'Nice view, not that I spent any time looking at it.'

Docklands was dark below. Tower Bridge twinkled. Above Corey, the red and green landing lights of a plane going into Heathrow flashed rhythmically, diminishing into the west.

'Okay.' She turned round. 'What do you want me to do?'

The white-haired man looked faintly amused. With his coat off, and his black tie undone, it was apparent how wide his shoulders were for an old man, how broad his chest. With only the lights from the bedside lamp, his face was shadowed. He said, 'I thought it was your job to know.'

'Uh, yeah,' Corey said. After a moment's thought she unzipped her leather jacket and let it fall heavily to the floor. 'Right.'

He rasped, 'You're not a whore.'

Corey opened her mouth. No words came out. She shrugged.

'No,' she said at last.

'You're not even one of Serena's high-class hustling friends.' His West Coast accent had deepened.

'No.'

Part of her rudeness came, she realised suddenly, from regret. She had sat thigh to thigh with him in his chauffeur-driven limousine on the way to his apartment, and something in the warmth of his flesh, the very male smell of him, had surprised her with its attractiveness. Under other circumstances . . .

'A friend of mine dared me to do it for money. So what?' Corey asked.

'So that makes you a very foolish young woman, and a waster of my time,' the big old man growled. 'Or else . . .' He paused. 'Or else it makes you a very naughty little girl.'

The apartment bedroom was hot. I thought it was supposed to be air-conditioned, Corey thought wildly. A strange warmth began to burn in the pit of her stomach. She looked around at the wide bed, the drinks bar, the tv/voicemail screen in its cabinet, the stomach-turning panoramic window. A soft silence enfolded the room, making it somewhere apart from the rest of the apartment building, apart from the rest of the world.

Corey swung around and faced the craggy, white-haired man. She put her leather-gloved fists on her hips, and her head to one side. 'So I'm a naughty girl. So what happens to naughty little girls?'

'*This.*'

35

He stepped in close before she could move. She had an instant to smell his expensive aftershave and stare at his spotless white shirt front. Then he reached and grabbed one of her wrists in each of his hands, pushed them behind her back, and transferred his grip on both her wrists to one hand.

He was strong, but old. She could have broken the grip.

He jerked her wrists. She spun until she faced half away from him. His hand lifted her wrists, forcing her forward. Her hair fell into her eyes as she bent, head and shoulders down.

A movement caught her eye. In the uncurtained glass, her reflection was plain against the black night. A skinny, ragged-skirted young woman with booted feet apart on the carpet, bent over forwards, bottom up; and behind her the strong old man, a shadow of white shirt and black tailored trousers.

He lifted her wrists higher. 'Missy, I'll show you what happens to bratty little girls!'

Her upper body was forced down. When he pushed, she was forced to stagger forward. He marched her to one of the plush armchairs, and sat on one arm of it. His strong grip thrust her forward and she sprawled across his lap.

Her balance was gone, her feet off the floor. Head hanging down, hair in her eyes, she squirmed and wriggled, trying first to slide off forward, then backwards, but his grip on her was surprisingly tight.

He ran his free hand over her rump.

She stiffened with the suddenness of it. His palm caressed the thick lace folds of her skirt. Then, with a sudden movement, he flicked her skirt up from her waist, over her shoulders. She squirmed, her bottom up.

Corey felt his fingers under the waistband of her

leggings and panties, tugging them down. The room's suddenly cool air slid over her bare buttocks. His hand removed itself. Pushed against his chest and thighs, she could feel his breathing quicken.

'Bad girl!'

A sharp hand stung her across both buttocks.

Corey yelped in surprise. Reflex action made her struggle. She got one foot to the floor, pushed, and felt his grip on her wrists loosen.

She hesitated for a split second.

The flat-handed blow still stung; she could feel the skin of her bare bottom glow. But the strange warmth in the pit of her stomach had been joined by a growing arousal between her legs. Startled beyond measure, she felt her pussy pulse wet.

Corey let the toe of her boot skid on the carpet. She fell forward again, across the man's thighs. Her unprotected bottom jutted up.

'Trying to get away, hah?' His voice rumbled in his chest. 'I reckon that makes you a real bad little girl.'

The hard hand came down again. This time it struck squarely, and she yowled. He drew his arm back. She wriggled, spreading her legs, arching her bottom up. The next spank caught her thighs and her outer labia.

'Ohhh!' She slid back in surprise. Her sex throbbed.

He dropped his hand between her torso and his body, tugging at the zip of his trousers. She pushed forwards. Her breasts in her tight bodice pressed into his lap, pushing against his hard, hot cock.

Two smart blows stung her left buttock and her right buttock. She squealed, experimentally at first, and then louder when he made no complaint. She felt his cock swell against her cleavage. She braced, getting both feet to the floor and straightening her legs. Her head dipped, and she mouthed the head of his thick, stubby cock.

'That—'

'Oh!'

'—is—'

'*Oh!*'

'—bad!'

'Ohhh!'

His calloused hand slapped hard on to her buttocks.
A fire exploded. She clamped shut on his hand as she
came, taken by surprise. He stood up, spilling her on
to the carpet, and delivered one last swat to her
stinging backside.

As her breathing quietened, she lay and watched her
own sprawled reflection in the black of the glass
window.

'May I?' The old man knelt beside her, holding out a
glass with a finger of whiskey in it. When she took it,
he swung around, stiffly, and sat beside her on the
floor, his back against the arm of the armchair. His
white hair was streaked with sweat. It fell over his blue
eyes in surprisingly boyish licks.

'That was most enjoyable,' he said. 'I hope you had
no objection.'

'I could have stopped you,' Corey admitted, 'if I had
any objections.'

'My old man used to lay into me with a leather belt
when I was a kid,' the man drawled reminiscently.
'Don't suppose he had the slightest idea what he was
startin'.'

'My family didn't believe in spanking children.'
Corey sipped the whiskey. It went down smoothly.
'I'm twenty-two. The only time I've seen a man spank
an adult woman is in old nineteen-fifties cowboy
films.'

'I have a video copy of every one,' he said gravely. 'I
shall get my chauffeur to drive you to your home,
young lady.'

Corey rolled over and sat up. The thick plush carpet was soft under her bare bottom. She rolled her leggings down and slipped them off, separated her skimpy panties out from the bundle, and turned her back to pull them on and up.

'You didn't come,' she said, kneeling facing away from him, but watching his reflection in the window.

One of his rough white eyebrows quirked up. 'What are you saying?'

Corey looked over her shoulder and grinned. 'I came but you didn't. I guess that makes me naughty.'

'Missy, I can see that it does.'

'But you'll have to catch me first!'

She intended to run behind the far side of the bed. As she sprang up, he reached forward with startling speed and grabbed her ankle. She sprawled full length on her face on the plush carpet.

Before she could get up, a hand grabbed her belt at the small of her back and lifted her.

'Bad girl!'

His hands pinned her wrists in the small of her back. She felt him grope under her stomach, at her belt-buckle. The leather strap suddenly jerked tight, then loosened, and the belt fell away from her unprotected waist. He caught the buckle and belt-end, doubling it into a thick leather loop.

Once again she felt herself thrust forward over his knee, as he sat down spread-legged on the bed. She pushed forward. Her straining breasts slid on the skin of his thighs, pushed out of the top of her bodice. 'Why am I bad?'

His stubby cock hardened under her body. 'Because you creamed your little panties, missy. *Bad!*'

A hard smack with the leather belt emphasised his words. A rain of blows struck her buttocks, so fast and so sharp that she could not count, only writhe and squeal. She thrust her body up to meet the blows of her own belt. He would not pull her panties down this time. The silky fabric between her legs became soaked with her juices, hot with her desire, until she was twisting and moaning, pushing her mound into his hard-muscled leg. Each blow on her reddened buttocks stung more hotly.

Abruptly he dropped the belt and lifted her, threw her forward on to the bed, rolled her over on to her back, and pulled down her panties. She saw his thick, stubby cock push between her spread thighs, against her hot sex.

'Now!' she screamed. 'Come on, come on, come on, *now*—'

The thick head of his cock pushed into her. She widened her legs and took him, clamping down on him as soon as he was inside her. She gripped his lean buttocks, pulling him down, banging his body into hers, until she felt his hot seed suddenly explode into hcr, and with that she yelled shrilly and came, her sex convulsing, pushing him back outside with her strength and fire.

'Oh, shit!' she said dizzily. 'That was – that was – that *was*.'

His hot, heavy, bony body sprawled heavily across hers. He lay and panted. Then he lifted a sweat-streaked, lined and wrinkled face, and gave her that smile that was forty years younger than he was.

'I had no idea,' Corey added.

'Missy, I envy you. You have so many years to make use of what you know.'

She stroked his face. 'And you've had so many years.'

'Sure have, missy. And there's a good few left in me yet.'

By the morning, when the chauffeur at last came

and she was woken from her sleep with one arm over the old man's broad shoulder, she stumbled into her clothes, half asleep before her first cup of coffee.

'You did say it was a dare, missy,' his strong voice rumbled.

'Oh – yes. Oh, give me a token five cents or something. That should still count as doing the dare.' She smiled at him muzzily.

Not until she was in the chauffeur-driven limousine did she feel something bulky against her side, and took out from the inside pocket of her leather jacket a thick white envelope.

The lunch-time rain had eased, and the Café Valletta emptied. Music played, over-loud now that the café had few people in it. Strong sun through the windows began to warm the skin of Shannon Garrett's bare arms.

She reached down and prodded the fat envelope. 'What are you going to do with the money?'

'Mmm?' Corey came back from her reverie. 'Oh – I don't know yet. Haven't thought.'

Shannon stood reluctantly. 'I suppose I'd better get back to the office. I'm late. Corey, that was . . . you . . .'

The younger woman shook her head. 'I just keep thinking about it! I tell you, Shannon, I'd do it again if I had the chance.'

'We couldn't possibly do it again,' Shannon protested.

'Scared?' Corey looked up, her eyes an incredibly deep blue in her clear-skinned face.

'No- . . .'

Nadia Kay stubbed out a thin cigarette. 'I don't know when I last felt so *alive*. Shannon, don't leave yet. I have an idea, as I said when I last spoke to you on the phone.'

'I'm not going to like this.' Shannon Garrett stood looking down at the two friends whom she had dared. 'Am I?'

Nadia leaned back in her chair. Corey, now apprehensive, sat up and looked at the older woman.

'Well . . .' Nadia tucked a red-gold curl back behind her ear. She removed her sunglassees and gazed across at the two of them.

'First, Corey dared you, Shannon. And then you dared Corey – and dared me as well. *I* haven't had a turn. I think, to be fair, that I should dare each of you, now. This game isn't over yet.'

Chapter Four

MUSIC LEAKED FROM next door through the living-room wall of Shannon Garrett's terraced house. It was audible even over the television. Shannon sighed. *After all the yelling I did at Tim, I don't think I can complain. Not for a while.* She felt for the remote control, and knocked the early evening news soundtrack up a notch.

She didn't take the world news in.

'Well, Shannon, how was *your* day?' she asked herself. Her voice sounded flat in the empty living-room. 'Last week I broke up with my married lover, then I went for lunch with my friends, went back to the office, made a few phone calls, got on with the job, left early. Oh, and I picked up a total stranger and fucked him. And I loved it!'

Cars went by outside in the narrow east London streets. A bee buzzed in from the open kitchen door and flew in rapid circles before leaving.

I can't believe I said that!

She got up and went to the kitchen. *Too hot to cook.* She poured herself a glass of supermarket red. She looked back into her living room.

Right. Despite anything Nadia says, we've all done a

dare. It was very nice. Unfortunately, now it's back to the real world. I'll have to phone and tell her that. That I'm not coming round this evening to discuss it, even. It's ridiculous!

Shannon put the glass down. She walked into the living-room. With the aid of a chair, she reached up and took down the framed Degas prints from the walls. Not much to show for six years.

Without warning, memories flashed in front of her eyes. Lunch-time sex. Her pussy heated. She had to put the last framed print down quickly before she dropped it.

I can't believe I did that in the first place. I certainly can't do it again! But if Nadia can think up a really inventive dare, will either of us feel able to back down? What am I *saying?* Shannon stopped and put her hands to her flushed face.

Back to the real world, I said. Or do I mean – I enjoyed it so much that it scares me?

Nadia's doorbell buzzed. When she looked out of her first-floor window, she saw Shannon standing expectantly on the pavement below. The younger woman was still in her work clothes, with her jacket slung over her arm.

'You got here, then.'

'Uh – yes. I guess.'

Nadia leaned out and looked up and down the street. 'I thought you and Corey were coming together?'

Shannon Garrett shrugged. She looked vaguely embarrassed. 'I thought so too.'

'She won't let us down.' The scent of roses filled Nadia's nostrils, from her window-box. Her side-street was deserted in the evening sun. At the end, where it opened into Baker Street, hundreds of sweating commuters still thronged the pavements.

'Come up.' Nadia triggered the ground-floor door lock. 'I have some iced tea ready.'

She went into the flat's tiny kitchen and emerged with a tray and glasses, which she put on the table in her main room. The white walls were disproportionately high for the room's width, but she loved her Edwardian conversion flat, even if it wasn't really big enough for both herself and all the *Ephemera* stock not currently displayed in the shop.

Voices sounded on the stairs outside the door, one of them Shannon's. When Nadia opened the front door, Corey tumbled in too, panting. Her black hair was slicked up with the heat, and her usually pale cheeks were pink with exertion. Her black cotton summer dress was crumpled.

'I ran all the way from the Tube station!' Corey flung herself down on the sofa nearest the open window. 'Sorry. Got stuck on the phone as I was coming out. Patricia! I'm not even *married* to her limp-dick son any more. Men!' She seized a glass of iced lemon tea and gulped it down, the frosting on the glass melting over her fingers.

Shannon looked around, obviously searching for somewhere to hang her jacket that was not already taken up by 1920s antique clothing.

'Put it in the bedroom,' Nadia said, 'then come and sit down.'

'You've got them, haven't you?' the brown-haired woman said as she came back into the room. 'Your dares. I can't believe I'm doing this. . .'

'You don't have to do it if you don't want to.'

'Stop treating us like babies!' The black-haired girl sprawled back on the sofa. She crossed her long legs at the ankles, and folded her arms over her ample bosom. Her eyes were brilliant with excitement. 'And I bet you've made them easy – because you think we won't do them otherwise!'

Nadia put her glass of iced tea down. 'Really, Corey.'

'Oh, I'm sorry. I'm just crabby because of Patricia. I prefer to forget Ben.' Corey smiled winningly. 'You've got a right to your turn to dare us. But I want a proper *competition* – let's see if Shannon and I can do the *same* dare, and see who does it best.'

'She's got a point,' Shannon said, turning back from the window. 'How can we say who wins? We need an objective judge. Not one of us. We could – oh, I don't know. Tell the dares as hypothetical stories to someone.' She paused. 'What about Michael?'

You've thought this out beforehand, Nadia smiled to herself. 'As a gay man, he certainly should be objective. Shannon, my dear, I take it this means that you are doing another dare?'

The brown-haired woman licked her lips. A scent of perfume and faint sweat came off her in the heavy summer's air. She took a deep breath and smiled. 'Like I said. I can do anything you two can do.'

Nadia held out a folded slip of paper. Shannon took it. 'Good grief, Nadia, you have *got* to be joking!'

Nadia smiled. She said softly, 'I dare you.'

Shannon wiped the palm of her hand down her linen skirt.

'Show it to Corey,' Nadia added, 'since you both want the same dare this time.'

The black-haired girl sprang up and leaned to read over Shannon Garrett's shoulder. 'Oh, what! Nadia, I bet *you've* never done that!'

'I'm sure the winner will be equally inventive when it comes to my turn.' Nadia smiled. 'I shall expect you for supper in, shall we say, a week?'

Corey bounced on the sofa. 'It's Wednesday today. Let's make it Friday evening. Thanks for the tea, Nadia, I'm off!'

There was a minute's silence after the girl had gone. The sound of the slammed door and footsteps down the stairs echoed. Nadia heard Corey Black whistling as she walked up the road.

Nadia glanced at Shannon. The brown-haired woman had her head bent over the paper scrawled over with Nadia's unkempt handwriting. She absently rubbed her fingers against her chilled glass, and then stroked the cold moisture against the back of her neck and behind her ears. Her upper lip was beaded with sweat.

'I wonder why Patricia is calling Corey again?' Shannon said absently. 'She didn't like the girl when she *was* her mother-in-law, so why she should call after the divorce. . .'

'Oh, I think they're still waiting for the decree absolute.' Nadia savoured the icy tang of the lemon tea on her tongue. 'Mmm. Friday evening. That doesn't give you a lot of time. I shall invite Michael. You'll be there, Shannon – won't you?'

Shannon Garrett looked up, her expression something between arousal and terror. 'Will I?' she said.

'No,' Shannon said. 'I won't be in today, Arabella. No, there's nothing that needs doing before Monday. Have the subs finished with that piece on nightclubs?'

She talked with her assistant for a few more minutes. Then she folded up the mobile phone and replaced it in her briefcase on the café table. The music of Covent Garden buskers echoed down from the high glass roofs. A pigeon fluttered past her head, one wing skimming her hair. She flinched. Her heart raced.

It's Friday. I don't even have a whole day left! If I don't move fast, I'm going to lose. They'll say I copped out. They'll think I couldn't do it!

Nadia's dare was succinct. *I dare you to fuck two or*

more strangers together.

The crotch of her silk panties grew damp as she visualised it. Shannon shifted in her seat.

How do I find someone – more than one – who's willing? How do I do this!

As she sat up, she gazed around the open-air cafe. Tourists. Men in jeans and T-shirts, women in pastel cottons. Shannon let her glance stray to the crotches of worn, soft denim jeans.

I might pick one who doesn't speak English!

She giggled, and smothered it in a cough. A man looked up from the next table, caught her eye, and continued his conversation with a colleague while he held her gaze for several seconds.

She felt one of her high-heeled sandals slipping off her foot. She bent down to adjust it. Her silk blouse, unbuttoned at the top, momentarily fell open as she leaned forward. The lace of her bra and the soft warm cleft between her breasts became visible.

Slowly, Shannon sat up again.

The man's gaze moved up to her face.

Two men were sitting at the next table. The one who held her gaze seemed forty-ish, but no older than that. A definite air of authority clung to him. Expertly manicured and shaved, extremely well-dressed. When he turned back to his conversation she let her eyes stray up his back. The suit was well-tailored to his lean body. She caught a scent of expensive aftershave, and under it a hint of male sweat.

The man with him was younger, broad-shouldered, and fair-haired. His suit jacket was thrown over the back of his chair. Sweat marked his shirt under his arms. He appeared harassed. Papers and electronic diaries were strewn across the table between the two men.

As she watched, the older man leaned back and smiled with an expression of utter control.

I know how I do this, Shannon thought. I know exactly how I do this.

Her mouth was dry with anticipation as she stood. Automatically she smoothed down her silk-lined linen skirt. She slung her jacket off one shoulder. And as she passed their table, a hidden flick of her thumb triggered her briefcase catch.

'Oh!' Papers spilled at her feet and across the men's table. 'Oh, I'm so sorry!'

'Please, don't mention it.' The older businessman scooped up papers and handed them to her as she crammed them into her case. He leaned back in his chair. Again, his bright eyes met hers. Laughter lines creased the corners of his eyes. 'Actually, James and I were about done here. Could I perhaps buy you a drink?'

Shannon let the pause hang in the air. The younger man, his cheeks slightly flushed, muttered something apologetic and made as if to rise. Shannon sat down on one of the chairs, blocking his way.

'I'd love to,' she confessed. 'It would be a shame to go back to the office on a day like this. Let's have some wine.'

'Edward—' The younger man seemed anxious.

The dark-haired man waved expansively. He had a long, rangy body which his well-cut suit emphasised. 'We can take a long lunch, I believe.' He still kept his eyes on her face. Shannon moved her shoulders back slightly. Her breasts pressed against the silk of her blouse.

The fair-haired man, James, sat back down. His blond eyebrows gave his face a permanent appearance of startlement. 'Oh. Oh, right. I know a little pub near here. It has a garden at the back,' he suggested. 'It usually isn't as crowded.'

Shannon nodded. 'Then take us there.'

She and Edward followed the fair-haired man through the Covent Garden crowds. She was electrically conscious of the older man walking behind her. When the packed tourists' bodies pressed them together, she felt the lean muscle of his thigh press once, lightly, against her buttock. She did not pull away. The chatter and calls made speech impossible. She looked over her shoulder at him and did not smile.

His face was equally impassive.

Some streets away, they entered a pub. Shannon found herself half-blind in the bar, after the sunlight outside. She did not wait to hear what James ordered. She moved towards the open door at the rear.

The high heels of her sandals made her conscious of her walk. They thrust her buttocks and breasts slightly out, for balance. Her skin flushed suddenly warm, knowing she was commanding their attention.

'Through here,' the older man said, his voice educated and controlled. She moved, conscious of his gaze, out into a walled courtyard where traffic noise was almost inaudible, and faint music played in the background.

'I ordered Pimm's, and champagne.' The blond young man was flustered, sweating in his suit jacket. Shannon smiled and sat down on a wooden bench. She patted the seat beside her. After a moment's hesitation, he sat down.

'What's your name?' he blurted.

'Elaine,' she replied without hesitation. It was her second name: Shannon Elaine Garrett.

'If you don't mind,' James said, 'I'll take my jacket off.'

'Why not.' Edward removed his own suit jacket and put it over the back of his chair, which he had drawn up to the end of the table. 'It really is very hot indeed.'

They talked inconsequentially. Towards three

o'clock, Shannon realised the pub garden had been deserted for at least an hour.

'I'm afraid if we want any more, we shall have to go in and order it,' the older man, Edward, said. 'They won't come out.'

Shannon glanced up at the windowless brick walls that surrounded them, masked by green creepers in which bees lazily buzzed. The scent of honeysuckle cut through the air, sweet in her nostrils.

The dark-haired man leaned back in his chair with an air of authority, his legs wide apart. The fly of his trousers had a definite bulge. Patches of sweat darkened the underarms of his shirt. He smelt very male now. Despite his increasing laughter, Shannon had watched him enough to know that he had drunk very little alcohol since they arrived. He watched her.

As if oblivious, she sat up on the wooden bench. With a completely erect posture, she slid her linen jacket back off her shoulders and let it fall to the ground. She smoothed her hands over her silk shirt, down her breasts, to her flat stomach.

'Edward, I think I should be getting back,' James stuttered nervously. He was not much older than Shannon. She caught his gaze, looking deep into his pale blue eyes, and held it for a long moment.

'Don't break up the party.' Her voice was husky now. James had a fit body, a squash-player's body. She admired the play of muscles on his forearms as he rolled his shirt sleeves up. Tiny golden hairs caught the sun. Light flashed from the heavy metal band of his watch.

Shannon sat back. The hem of her skirt rucked up, showing the tops of her sheer stockings, and a suspender.

'I always think stockings are cooler than tights in this heat,' she remarked. 'But I am still very hot.'

She was completely sober. More glasses of wine had gone into the grass beside the table than down her throat. She wriggled her skirt down over her knees. 'I could always take them off, couldn't I.'

'You could take them off, Elaine,' Edward said. A faint line of sweat shone on his forehead.

Of course I will, Shannon thought with a sense of complete freedom. I'm 'Elaine', I can do whatever I want, and I'll never see these men again.

'But it would be a shame,' the younger man added hastily. 'I've always liked stockings myself – on a woman, that is – I mean—'

'But it's so hot.' Shannon reached up and unbuttoned another blouse button. The cream silk clung to her damp skin. If she moved at all now, her blouse would fall open.

Deliberately, she shifted around on the bench. Slowly she extended one leg on to the grass, her toe pointed. Sheer stockings glimmered in the sun. Slowly she put her fingers either side of her knee and began to slide them upwards. Her skirt began to ruck up.

'Very hot. . .'

Now her fingers glided over the top of her stockings, on to the cool flesh of her upper thigh. Her skirt rode up to expose one suspender.

Her body leaning forward made her blouse fall open. The silk material fell away. The full curve of her breasts, contained by her lace and silk bra, shone in the sunlight. A fine sweat pearled her cleavage. Without lifting her body, she raised her eyes to the men sitting either side of her.

'I – ah – ought to go,' James's voice squeaked beside her. He was holding his briefcase on his thighs, concealing his lap.

Shannon shifted her gaze to the older, dark-haired man, Edward. She unsnapped one suspender, and dropped her gaze from his face to his crotch. His face was impassive. A huge erection strained at the fly of his suit trousers. The dark cloth outlined a thick, long cock. He made no attempt to conceal his arousal.

'James,' she said, 'help me with these.'

'Um—'

'These.' Her fingers slid her skirt up on the outside of her thigh, exposing another white suspender. 'Come and help me undo this. There's a good boy.'

Edward gave a deep chuckle. It might have been that that made a steely determination come into the younger man's eyes.

He put the briefcase down on the table and knelt at her side.

His erection poked out the fly of his trousers. Shannon watched it harden and swell as he saw her looking at him. She slid her tongue-tip over her lips.

The wood of the bench was warm under her pussy. The crotch of her knickers dampened as she shifted, exposing more of the length of her leg. Mesmerised, the young fair-haired man took the suspender in his fingers and unsnapped it.

'There's one at the back.' Shannon straddled the bench and leaned forward until her belly and breasts pressed into the hard wooden surface. She reached behind herself and slid one hand over her skirt-waist, over her buttocks, until she could hitch up the hem of her skirt.

She turned back to lie face-down on the bench. Her breasts pushed up out of the neck of her blouse. They swelled with arousal, her bra now uncomfortably tight.

Her skin shivered as the young man's hard, warm fingers fumbled at the back of her thigh. She heard another suspender unsnap. After a second, she felt his hands begin to roll her stocking down her thigh.

The sun caressed her bare flesh. The scent of

honeysuckle was hot and heavy. She held the older man's gaze.

'Edward . . .' She stroked the lacy edge of one bra cup. 'It's so hot, and I'm *so* uncomfortable.'

'I find myself in some discomfort.' His voice was a rasp. He sat with a straight back, the picture of a proper businessman. He pointed, with an air of authority, at his crotch. 'Perhaps if I were – less uncomfortable. . .'

Shannon reached her hands out and grasped the end of the bench. She pulled herself along it on her belly. The hard wood pushed at her soft, aroused breasts. Her nipples swelled and hardened. Her engorged breasts strained at the now-painful constriction of her bra.

She felt cool air on her other thigh. The young man's hands fumbled at her suspenders there. Her hot skin shivered under his touch.

Now that she was leaning forward on the bench, her crotch was raised, and the bench was not pressing against it. She whimpered with anguish, pushing her buttocks back, but they came into contact with nothing except empty air.

'Do it . . .' She raised her head to look back over her shoulder. The blond man straddled the bench, straddled her where she lay face down. A tiny damp spot marked the crotch of his trousers, where his bulging concealed cock had wept a droplet of liquid. His sportsman's muscles tensed on his forearms.

Wanting, aching, Shannon pushed her toes against the earth. She raised her buttocks slightly from the bench, inviting. The crotch of her knickers was soaking wet.

'Do it!' she repeated.

She did not wait for him to act. Now that she lay with her head at the end of the bench, she could reach

Edward's chair. She put her hands on each side of his chair, and dropped her face into his lap.

'I'm going to suck you dry.' Her mouth was close to his fly. Her moist breath feathered his crotch. He grunted. Both his hands gripped the metal arms of the chair. Involuntarily, his hips jerked up. His crotch pressed into her face.

Shannon strained forward, the bench hard against her stomach and breasts. She mouthed his concealed cock through the fabric of his trousers. He gasped. Slowly she brought one hand forward and unbuttoned his top button. She took hold of the zip and tugged experimentally.

'Oh!' Cool air suddenly brushed her buttocks.

The unseen hands of the young man behind her caught either side of her skirt and rucked it up, wrenching it roughly, until it was around her hips. She felt him grab the back of her panties with his whole fist. There was a second of aching anticipation; then he jerked them down. The sheer fabric tore.

He thrust one hand between her legs, under her stomach. His hand, flat against her belly, felt huge. With one muscular movement he pulled her up from the bench and pressed her forwards.

Shannon's high-heeled sandals got a grip. Now she was resting only her upper torso and breasts on the bench. One hand gripped the dark-haired businessman's zip, the other steadied her against his chair.

The tip of a cock brushed her labia. She jerked, steadied, braced herself. With one single movement she yanked down the zipper on the dark-haired man's trousers. His thick cock sprang free. She plunged her face into the springy dark hair at the base of it. Her tongue dived into the sweaty crevices between his balls and his body. His hips raised. She pushed in, her hot tongue licking behind his balls, teasing the flesh

55

between his legs, tasting salt perspiration. She heard him groan. She mouthed her way back along his hairy upper thighs.

'Tell me what you're going to do,' he groaned. 'Talk dirty.'

'I'm going to suck you off. I'm going to take your big cock in my mouth and I'm going to suck and lick until you come in my mouth. And while I'm doing it, I'm going to tell your friend to fuck me from behind. He's going to fuck me hard. I'm going to suck you dry. Ahh!'

The younger man's hands gripped her waist. His stiff cock prodded her sex. She pressed back. The head of his cock pushed within her lips; withdrew: pushed in, withdrew; with a noise of sucking wetness.

Shannon slid her tongue from root to tip of Edward's cock, inhaling his musky smell. She glimpsed his white knuckles on the arms of his chair. Greedily she lowered her lips over him, taking him into her mouth, sucking first at the tip, then at the quiveringly aroused shaft. His hips began to pump upwards. Sweat stained his white shirt, rucked up out of his suit trousers; she glimpsed his flushed face and sweat-matted hair.

'I'm fucking you!' he groaned. 'James! Fuck Elaine. Fuck her hard. *Now*. Fill her right up!'

From behind her, James's cock slammed into her wet, aching sex. She paused for a split second on toe-tip, adjusting to the rhythm. Then, as he penetrated her from behind, she sucked Edward's cock in the same rhythm that James was fucking her. The thick shaft in her pussy and the thick shaft in her mouth were one thing, one experience; she held and was penetrated simultaneously, thrusting and sucking, thrusting and sucking. The rhythm of the cock swelling in her mouth and the cock fucking in her sex hypnotised her: minutes might have passed, or hours.

James's muscled thighs were hard against the back of

her legs. His hands gripped her body. His hips rammed into her buttocks. His balls banged against her. She felt herself open and flower hotly. The cock inside her mouth hardened, achingly erect, widening her lips.

Her pussy clenched, taking the man behind her deep inside. At the same moment she took the other man's cock deep into her throat. Above her Edward cried out and came, pumping strongly. The excitement of that fired her own orgasm, and as she clamped down on the man whose hips thrust into her buttocks, she heard James cry out as he shot his seed into her waiting sex. Drenched, sweat-soaked, she collapsed down on to the bench with her head in Edward's lap. The hard-muscled body of James slumped down across her back, his breath deep and panting. She experienced a moment of heat: sun, sexual bodies, sweat, semen, and the weight and touch of them both, both men satiated, pressing against her skin.

Her silk-lined skirt was creased, rucked up around her waist. Her blouse was undone. One breast had popped from its constricting bra-cup, the other was still enclosed in silk and lace. One stocking and one sandal had gone. The warm air felt like silk over her bare buttocks. Her panties were a ripped scrap of cloth laying on the grass beside the wooden bench.

Edward's tailored trousers were creased and dark with sweat, and spattered with come. His chest still rose and fell rapidly. She rested her cheek against his thigh. James's weight lay on her body and shoulders. When she glanced back, she saw him with the buttons popped off his shirt, and his suit trousers around his ankles. He wore red wool socks.

In summer! Shannon chuckled. Great body. Shame about the rest. She met his eyes and giggled again, deliciously satisfied. She feasted on the sight of his torso and thighs, and his limp and now-shrinking cock. Her nipples began to harden.

I never did get my breasts sucked, she thought dreamily. Now just let me tell them—

A nearby clock struck.

'Good grief!' Shannon exclaimed. She sat up, spilling the fair-haired man heavily on to the grass. He grunted and winced. She said, 'Is that the time? I have to go!'

Chapter Five

IN THE ENSUING silence, Nadia opened another bottle of wine. Michael Morgan allowed her to fill his glass. He was a young, plump man, elegant as ever in blue jeans and a tailored shirt.

'That was some story, Shannon,' he said admiringly. 'I know straight men who'd find that a real turn-on.'

'Freely adapted from some of the letters we get into the office,' Shannon Garrett said blandly.

Nadia caught her eye and grinned.

'What about mine now?' Corey's voice sounded muffled. The tall girl knelt on the wide window-sill. She peered down into the street. Then she straightened, still kneeling above the drop, and nodded. 'Yeah, I can see it. My bike's OK. It's only a Honda 350, and it's older than God, but it's all mine and I love it.'

Michael raised his glass. 'How about a biker story? That might be even more to my taste.'

'Funny you should say that, Mike.' She sat down and switched her legs into the room. 'I could tell mine like it happened. Like it happened to me, I mean. Shall I?'

'I love a story competition.' He drained his wine and

held the glass out to Nadia. 'Do start.'

The girl put one foot up on the sill. Nadia watched her lean her back against the window's edge. She was wearing an extra-long T-shirt borrowed from Nadia, over bra and knickers. Her leathers were hung up inside the bathroom door, that being the only free hook.

'Right.' Corey smoothed her short tangled black hair back from her face. 'What time is it? Let's say . . . about twenty-four hours ago. I was riding the bike back from a shoot in the Midlands. It was almost dark. You know what it's like riding a bike in summer, you get sweaty as hell underneath leather. So I pulled into one of the service stations, I don't know which.'

'No corroborative detail?' Michael queried.

'If I did, and got it wrong, you'd know. Are you telling this story or me? Shut up: it's going to be really good.' She swung her leg down from the sill and came back to the table, plumping down in the seat between Nadia and Michael, looking at them with bright eyes.

'You have to imagine I'm looking for a good fuck. I'm after my prey. And I don't just want one man. One man isn't enough this time.

'So anyway, I pulled the bike into this service station. There was just a bit of orange left in the west, but otherwise the sun had set. The sky overhead was dark. All the service station lights were on. I didn't recognise the place very well.

'Then I realise why I wouldn't recognise it anyway. I've missed my turning, and I haven't come into the bike and car park. I'm round where the lorries and the commercial vehicles park. That's why everything looks different. Once I get my helmet off I see it's a big badly-lit expanse of concrete with the lights of the petrol pumps way off in the distance. I can still hear the cars on the motorway, and I can smell engine oil, and diesel, and the food cooking in the service station café. But it looks like I've parked about a mile away from anywhere or anybody.

'This doesn't look good, I think. I'd been planning to go into the service area and see if I could find a couple of men on their own. Only there isn't anyone all the way out here.

'Just as I'm thinking that I'll have to kick the bike into life again, and go and park in the proper place, there's this roar of an engine, and these incredibly bright halogen headlights hit me in the eyes. I'm dazzled! I put my hand up to shield my face.

'A voice calls out, "Stay where you are, sir!"

'They haven't seen I'm a woman, whoever they are, because I'm in my leathers. Even with the helmet off I've got pretty short hair. Speaking of the leathers, I want to take them off by this time, because I'm getting really sweaty being in them without the slipstream from driving the bike. I don't know what to do, so I just stand still. The headlights go dim, but that doesn't help me, I'm still dazzled.

'The next thing I know, someone grabs me by the shoulders and pushes me round, and shoves me up against some kind of vehicle that I hadn't even seen in the darkness. Someone takes my hands and puts them on the vehicle's roof. What feels like a boot kicks my feet apart, so I have to stand straddled and leaning forward. Then some man's hand pats down my arms and up my legs.

'This voice says, "He's clean. And he's cute!" Then this hand just goes up between my legs and hits my crotch, and all of a sudden he snatches it away like it's on fire.

'I turn round. By this time my eyes have recovered. I can see that what I'm standing next to is a dark jeep, and that the man in front of me is dressed in light and

61

dark brown camouflage jacket and trousers. I can see just well enough in the twilight to tell that he's really blushing.

' "Uh, sorry, ma'am," he says. "I didn't realise."

'I realise he's got an American accent. He's a big man, about six foot two or three, and very broad across the chest. What I can see of his hair is bright blond, but it's shaved so close it just looks like fuzz.

'Another American voice says, "What is it, Gary?" A second soldier comes around the side of the jeep. I realise why I didn't see him at first. He's African American. And this black guy stands about four inches taller than the white guy. He looks at the bike and he looks at me. He's interested. Then he looks again. I can see him look down at my leathers, at my chest, and then at my face again.

'There are lots of military vehicles, now my eyes have got adjusted. Some kind of convoy? These two seem to be the only men with the vehicles. Both enlisted men, not officers. I think the others must be inside eating.

'I look at the second man. I can tell he's fit, as well as big; he's got real muscles. "Parked in the wrong place, huh?" he says.

'This black guy isn't wearing a battledress jacket, just camouflage trousers and a three-quarter sleeve T-shirt in the same US camouflage pattern. Boy, does he fill out his clothes nicely! His hair is closely shaved too, but I think it's kind of a nondescript brown.

' "Perhaps I didn't park in the wrong place." The two of them look at each other, and then at me.

'The first man, Gary, says, "What do you want, ma'am?"

'I look him up and down slowly. I'm starting to get hot now. There's no one around, but I can't tell how long it'll be until any of the others come back. I look him right in the eye and say, "I want a man with a big hard cock in his pants. Big enough to satisfy me. Do you think you've got what it takes?'

'The expression of shock on his face is beautiful. I see the black guy fumbling around for his wallet. I know what he's thinking.

' "I don't want money," I tell them. 'I'm looking for a man who's man enough for me, and I haven't met him yet.'

'They start eyeing each other up. I know any second one of them is going to tell the other to get lost. I don't want a fight, and I don't want one of them to go.

'So I say to Gary, "Why don't you and your friend have a little competition? I'll take you both on. I bet neither of you can make me come.'

'I'm really hot in my bike leathers now. I can feel my T-shirt underneath is wringing wet with sweat. While they're just standing there dumbstruck I reach up and pull the zip on my jacket down. It falls open. The night air on my wet skin is cold. I look down and I can see the cotton material clinging to my breasts, outlining my nipples which are standing right up. I put my arms back and let the jacket slide off, and then I sling it over the bike together with the helmet.

'When I look up again, they're both staring at my breasts. I'm getting really hot in the crotch now. I'm ready to have one of them inside me. I say, "Well?"

'The black guy says, "Look, this is pretty strange, ma'am, and there's something we should tell you."

'His friend Gary says, "You're cute, but we're not really into any kind of fucking except one, ma'am. But if you can take it up the ass, we're your men."

'I put my hands on my hips and stare them up and down. I say, "I can take anything you can give out, but you wimps aren't going to, are you?"

'As I planned, that does it. The big guy, Gary, steps

forward and grabs my hands. He twists my wrists into the small of my back, and turns me round, and marches me to the front of the jeep. My biker boots are skidding on the tarmac but I can't get any purchase – I don't really want to, but I'm not going to tell them that! I can tell my struggling is getting them excited. When I push back against Gary he's got a huge hard-on in his pants. It's getting *me* excited too, my pussy is sopping wet.

'Gary is immensely strong. When he pushes me face-down over the bonnet of the jeep, he can hold me there with just one hand. I can't push my body up, and he's holding my wrists behind my back. While I'm face down, I feel *another* hand – it's the second soldier, the black guy. He's kneeling beside the jeep and putting his hand up between my legs. I clamp my legs together but that's not what he's after. He reaches under my stomach for the fastenings of my leather jeans. I feel him pull down the zip. The leather is suddenly loose around my hips and thighs.

'Someone's hard-on pushes against my leg. I want to cry out, but I can't get my breath. Suddenly my wrists are released. Gary pushes my arms out stretched across the bonnet.

' "Hold on, ma'am," he says. "I'm gonna give it to you right up your pretty little ass."

' "I'm not ready!" I say, and I look over my shoulder while I hang on to the jeep bonnet for dear life. As I look, I see the black soldier. He's got a hand scooped full of something dark and sticky which in a moment I recognise as engine grease. I feel them both moving behind me, and one of them pulls my panties down, and the other slaps a handful of grease up between the cheeks of my buttocks.

'It's cold! But I don't cry out. Both their hands are working into my crack. Soon it's warm. I feel strong fingers circling my arse, teasing the edge of my hole, working the grease into it, making it flexible. I drive my hips against the metalwork of the vehicle. If I could rub my pussy against one of their legs I would come like a dog. I can't bear how hot I'm getting.

'Two greasy hands slide up under my wet shirt and grab my breasts. My nipples are so hard they're tender. Whoever it is massages my breasts until I think I'll go crazy. Then he says, 'She's ready, Johnnie.'

'The hands pull out from under me. I sprawl on the metal bodywork of the vehicle. A man's finger is inserted gently into my anus. It slides in and out, in and out, slowly at first, then faster and faster as I get looser. Soon it's not one finger, it's two. I don't know if they belong to Gary or Johnnie or both men together. I bend further forward.

'Two big hands grab my hips. The hot flesh of a cock-head nudges at my anus. At first it's not able to enter. Then I relax and with a sudden rush it goes in, past my sphincter muscle, and I'm pushed open. The front of my body comes up off the jeep and I brace myself bending forward, gripping with my hands. The man's cock thrusts up my arse and almost lifts me off the ground. Pulsations of heat are running through me. I've been bottom-fucked once before but it's never felt like this. I feel totally helpless.

'He thrusts again, and I'm lifted up on to tiptoes. I can feel his thick shaft rammed up my bottom. I look over my shoulder. As I thought, it's Gary. I can see his belly pressed up against my buttocks, and when he withdraws, I see the glistening shaft of his cock.

'Then I see Johnnie come and stand behind Gary. He's got another handful of that engine grease, and a wicked grin. He undoes Gary's pants and pulls them down around his ankles. Gary doesn't even break the rhythm of his thrust. When Johnnie slams the engine grease between the white guy's legs, his thrust lifts me right off the ground for a second. I'm so wet between my legs I just want something in there, anything. My ass feels so full, I know I'm going to come anyway, any second.

'Johnnie takes hold of the big soldier from behind and bends him over me. Gary's body is hot and heavy. He smells of the open air, and of oil and machinery. I can *feel* the thrust as the black soldier enters Gary. Gary's cock swells inside me until I think I can't take it, but I do. I look over my shoulder and see that I am being fucked up the arse by a big crew-cut blond soldier, who himself is being fucked up the arse by an even bigger black soldier. Their arms glisten with sweat. Their muscles stand out hard and taut. Johnnie reaches right forward past Gary and grabs my breast in his big hand. He squeezes so hard.

'Just that and the sight of them both fucking each other and I lose control. I explode. I come and I come, and I clench so hard that I squeeze Gary's cock right out of my arse. He falls on top of me as Johnnie finishes him with a mighty thrust, and Johnnie comes in Gary's arse, and I roll over and take him so that Gary comes in my hands.

'Then I'm sitting with my back against the side of jeep, on the oily concrete. The concrete is gritty and cold under my bare cheeks. My leathers are round my ankles. The night air is cooling my soaked T-shirt. These two huge guys are leaning either side of me, panting. The blond one's face is running with sweat.

'Then his friend Johnnie says, ''Hey, I thought this was a competition.''

'He's got this deep, rich voice; it vibrates right down to my toes. I put my hand on his chest. It's huge. He isn't breathing hard, he's hardly broken sweat.

' ''Ready when you are, ma'am,'' he says.

'I look down at his camouflage pants. The fly is open. His black cock is lying out, half-limp, but as I look, it starts to swell up. He looks as big as Gary, if not bigger.

'Gary's balls are wrinkled and not very hairy. He's sitting the other side of me with his big hand around his dick. He's grinning too.

'I put my hands on their shoulders and I push myself up on to my feet. My knees are shaking. The lights of the service station are a long way off. There's no one around that I can see. Cars go whizzing past on the motorway about forty foot the other side of a chain-link fence.

'I lean over the front of the jeep again. The metal hood is cold now. The shock makes my nipples hard. I can feel myself getting wet again. I say, "What are you waiting for?"

'Johnnie walks around the jeep until he's standing on the opposite site, about eighteen inches from my face. "I want you to see what you're getting, ma'am. *All* of it."

'He starts pulling at his cock. He's circumcised. Thankfully, I see that while he's got a good nine inches, it's a bit narrow. For what he's going to do to me, that's ideal. I lie there, bare-arsed, over the hood of the jeep, and the black guy just stands there sliding the satin-black skin up and down his cock and getting harder and harder.

'Something pushes the cheeks of my bottom apart. Hot lips kiss my arse. I flatten my tits down on the bonnet, pushing my bum up, trying to spread my ass as wide open as I can. A hot big tongue darts into my anus. It pulls back, pushes in again; starts to thrust.

' "Hey, man, what you doing there?"

' "Just getting her ready for you, boy," Gary's voice says behind me. I hear him spit, and then he's rubbing the saliva around my anus. I can't help pushing back into his hand. I'm running hot again, I can feel my own juices on my thighs.

' "Stand aside," says Johnnie. I turn my head and watch as he walks around behind me. His cock juts out from his pants, hard and long. He puts his hands on my bum. 'Ma'am, I got something here for you.'

'I say, "Let me have it!"

'His hands lift my hips and spread my cheeks. The air's cold. The circumcised head of his cock nuzzles at the entrance to my ass.

' "Coming up!" he says, and he shoves it right in. If Gary hadn't loosened me up, I couldn't take it. I feel like I'm being filled right up. I can feel every inch of that cock pushing up inside me. The ring of muscle at my entrance pricks and tingles, and then it doesn't hurt any more. It's getting me really hot.

'There's a heavy pair of hands on my shoulders, pushing me down. Gary's voice says, "Go, boy!"

'While Gary holds me down, the black soldier draws his cock back, then thrusts it up my arse. I feel like I want to lift right off the ground. Push and back, push and back; and my arse swells wide open to take the root of his cock as he jams it up me, shrinks as he draws away, and opens wide as his pile-driving body thuds forward.

'Gary doesn't have his hands on my back any more. I'm panting hard, the breath whistling between my teeth, and I'm trying not to yell or groan, someone might hear us. I look over my shoulder.

'The big blond soldier is down on his knees behind Johnnie. He's got both hands on those taut black cheeks, spreading them, and his face is jammed up in the crack, tonging Johnnie's arsehole like there's no tomorrow. I feel Johnnie groan: it vibrates inside me. My pussy is swelling hot. My arse is so full I can't bear it.

'Gary stands up and drops his camouflage pants again. He takes out his thick cock. It's purple at the head, engorged and erect. Johnnie says, "Oh man, don't do that, man, you're gonna take my mind off my work!"

' "Do it!" I gasp. "Fuck *him* while he's fucking me!"

'Slow and sure, Gary moves in behind the black guy. This time it's the black guy's turn to be pushed forward over me. I can feel his body running with sweat, it soaks into my T-shirt. He's heavy, and hard, and his whole body *jolts* as Gary sticks it in him.

'That's too much for me. I come again, and again, and then I stick my hand down underneath me on to my clit and come for a third time. I feel his cock shoot it's whole load up me. He fills me right up. Slippery come starts oozing out of me. My body bucks up under Johnnie but I can't shift his weight, so I come again right there under him.

'Gary's body thuds into both of us. The black guy juts his ass up as Gary takes him, and Gary shoots *his* load.

'My knees are shaking so much that I just slide down off the jeep's bonnet and lie there, in a tangle, these two big guys half on top of me, half sprawled over the concrete car park, in a panting heap.

'And when I stopped panting, I said, "Thanks, boys." And I pulled up my leather jeans, and put on my jacket and helmet, and I straddled my bike and I rode away.'

Nadia's flat smelled of vinegar, pasta sauce, and wine. The air was heavy, a storm close at hand. Nadia looked round at her three dinner companions; the two women with their elbows on the tables among the empty plates, in surprisingly similar poses; the man leaning back in his chair.

'Is my story better than hers?' Corey pointed at Shannon.

Michael Morgan's face had a dreamy look.

'That's the best.' He glanced around at the three women. 'I'm sorry: it is.'

'Just because it's got soldiers with big dicks in,' Corey teased.

'What I could tell you about the military, you wouldn't believe. No, knowing you, you might.' He smiled, turning to Nadia. 'Let me guess, that one was from a gay male porn film?'

'I don't know. Was it, Corey?' Nadia asked demurely.

'Something like that . . .'

'That's definitely the best story I've heard in a long time. Sorry, Shannon. Which reminds me,' he said, still slightly absently, 'I told Simon I wouldn't be late home tonight. If you ladies will excuse me . . .'

Not long afterwards, Nadia saw a slightly unsteady Michael to the door. She returned to a room of empty plates and glasses. Shannon had her feet resting on a second chair. Corey balanced one wine glass on top of another. Nadia walked over and took it away from her.

Corey grinned up at her. The young woman's clear blue eyes were bright in her pale face. 'I didn't get on the bike right away, actually. We hung around and got cleaned up and chatted. They were really nice. I won the dare, though, didn't I? I had both my guys.'

'I was interrupted!' Shannon protested. 'I didn't have enough time . . .'

Her face grew soft. Nadia saw her friend's habitual expression of slight primness vanish entirely.

'I know what it's like now,' Shannon continued, 'to just tell a man to fuck me. Or tell him I'm going to fuck him. You know what I thought, with Edward and James? I thought, this could be my best fuck ever.'

'Then the clock struck and you turned into a pumpkin.' Corey chuckled.

'I'd hardly got started. But I took the dare. I don't think I *did* lose,' the woman protested hotly. Her faintly freckled face flushed.

Corey grinned at her. 'Michael thinks you did.'

Nadia looked at the remnants of salad on dishes. *I ought to take those out to the kitchen.* She wore her green silk mandarin dress, and bronze sandals: the colours accentuated her copper-red hair. Her creamy skin glistened. *I'll clear up later. After – after I tell them. If I do.*

She crossed to the sash windows and pushed them up even further. 'Michael didn't hear all the stories.'

'What do you mean? Corey told hers, and I told mine.' Shannon's hazel eyes widened. 'What aren't you telling us?'

Nadia savoured the warm air on her face. The breeze did not stir the heavy curtains. Purple-blue clouds gathered over the roof-tops to the south, towards Oxford Street. Heat lightning flashed.

She said lightly, 'I thought I'd make it a real competition.'

Corey punched the air with her fist. 'Yes! You took your own dare!'

'You didn't!' Shannon exclaimed.

Nadia turned. Her eyes narrowed slightly, laugh-lines creasing at the corners. Her full lips smiled. 'I suppose I should have mentioned it to Michael before he judged between you two. I couldn't resist trying out my own dare – but sad to say, it went a bit wrong . . .'

Chapter Six

THURSDAY EVENING. NADIA handed her 1920s fur stole over at the cloakroom desk. As she turned away, she bumped into a tall, fair-haired man in evening dress.

'Um, Nadia, yes. There you are.' The man adjusted his bow-tie.

'Oscar. How very kind of you to invite me.' She let a touch of sarcasm enliven her tone.

He had the grace to look uncomfortable. 'You always used to like these dinners. I thought, well, Diane's away in the States, so . . .'

'So instead of bringing your wife, you'd invite your ex-wife. Innovative.' She smiled and linked her arm in his, having to look up. 'I do enjoy not being married to you any more, Oscar. When you're this insensitive, I can laugh at it.'

He chuckled unwillingly. She looked up at his strong, heavy brows and bewildered face. His thick, rough yellow hair had been chopped into an expensive neat cut.

And in two minutes, evening dress or not, he'll look like he's been dragged through a hedge backwards! Ah, but he's still the most good-looking man I know.

It's just such a *relief* not to want him any more.

'Shall we go in?' Oscar asked.

She squeezed his arm. They went together up the red plush stairs, under the white moulding and gilded scrolls. Nadia mentally priced the Victorian portraits of the Guild founders hanging on the walls. *Hardly investment quality, and I can't think of any other excuse for their existence . . .*

'Miss – Nadia – Kay,' the toast-master at the door boomed. 'Oscar – Trevithic.'

It was far from the first time she had been announced when she arrived at a function, but it still made her smile. Nadia paused on the stairs, looked across the heads of the crowd. The hot air seeping in from London outside made the big, barrel-vaulted hall stuffy. Men were monochromatically splendid in evening dress, women in sparkling sequins. Light glittered from silver cutlery on the spotless tablecloths, where the dinner would be served.

Nadia removed her arm from Oscar's and walked down the two steps into the hall with her head high. She wore moderately high heels, knowing that those and her sheer stockings showed her slim legs to best advantage. Her sheath dress of green satin was beaded from plunging neckline to split hem with tiny pearls and emerald sequins, 30s style. It fitted well enough that she could wear a garter belt and strapless bra without spoiling the line of it. She had styled her red hair into a neat Peter Pan cut, and wore two tiny green stone earrings.

'There's Carol,' she said, a practised moment before Oscar's hesitant discomfort became plain. 'I must go and say hello, I haven't seen her for ages. Be good, darling.'

'Darling, what a wonderful dress!' Carol kissed the air some two inches from Nadia's ear. 'Wherever did you get it?'

Car boot sale, Bodmin, and didn't I have to sleep the night in the MG in a car park to be there early enough? Or was that St Albans?

'It's rather exclusive, I'm afraid,' Nadia said airily.

Working the crowd took her some time. She was unlikely to see any of the contacts she had kept up after she divorced Oscar on any other occasion. Most of them knew of *Ephemera*. Some of them passed her hints and rumours of pieces for sale. By the time she sat down to eat, she was too busy calculating whether she could drive to Sheffield in time to look at a dealer's stock before he opened on Monday to note who she was seated next to.

She glanced around. Oscar sat on far side of the hall, between a blonde woman, and one in orange satin. A voice to her left said, 'Wine?'

'Mmm?'

A rather chunky, middle-aged man with grey hair, seated on her left, indicated the waiter.

'Oh, yes. Thank you.'

Nadia tasted her red wine. Passable.

'I'm Peter,' the middle-aged man continued. 'I'm in manufacturing.'

Nadia took another sip of the wine. The other man, on her right, seemed taken up with his companion to his right, an elegant academic-looking woman in her sixties. 'How interesting,' Nadia said gamely.

Before the end of the soup, she had learned rather more about producing widgets than she had ever wanted to know.

I could leave now, she thought. She leaned back as the bowls were removed. The hall had grown even hotter. Between the body heat of two hundred men and women, and the hot evening sun leaking in through the clerestory windows, she felt herself growing slick with sweat.

I've talked to everybody I want to talk to. I've talked to rather a lot of people I don't want to talk to. This chap Peter is very sweet, but I may hit him with the cruet well before dessert. Perhaps I could just put my hand up and say *Can I go home now, please?*

She beamed down at the glass in her hand. She had been twiddling it by the slender stem. It was empty again. I always drink too much when I'm bored. Oh damn.

And it's Friday tomorrow. I wonder if either of them will have . . . Or if both of them . . .

'You could talk to me,' a voice said, very quietly, to her right. 'I couldn't tell you the difference between a widget and a gadget. Or a Post-Modernist and a Post-Structuralist.'

Glancing past her dinner companion to the right showed Nadia the sixty-year-old academic woman deep in conversation with an African diplomat she vaguely recognised from a previous dinner.

She was conscious of an immediately physical attraction to the man sitting beside her. He was big. Not fat – a physically large body frame slabbed with muscle. And he smelled of something that tantalised her. Cinnamon? Patchouli? Sandalwood.

'Sandalwood.' His voice was deep. His arm next to hers at table had a certain bulk. 'On my hands. I had a shipment of incense to check through.'

She studied him. Like Oscar, a big man. You could never mistake him for a boy. Dark eyes surrounded by laughter-lines looked down at her. His brows were thick and dark. His hair was rough-textured, dark brown with a touch of silver. Good lord, he has big shoulders, Nadia thought. They strained his dinner jacket. She let her gaze move down his body, solid under the evening jacket.

His easy movement as he leaned back in his chair shifted the expanse of his shoulders. His body tapered only slightly from a barrel chest to solid hips. His legs when he crossed them were strong and well-muscled under the cloth of his evening trousers. He wore the formal clothing with complete ease.

He's not one of Oscar's circle. Not that class. Lower. Military? she wondered. Police officer? Perhaps. Some kind of non-civilian authority about him – under that politeness, he thinks he knows more about real life than anyone else at this table.

Her attraction was positive and growing. Nadia's fingers itched. She wanted to pull his tie undone. Undo the buttons on the stiff shirt. Rumple the neatly-pressed cloth of his evening jacket.

He'd look good stripped. Slow warmth stirred in her groin at the thought. Damn, I've a good mind to take on the other two at this. I wonder if he has a friend?

'Here.' He refilled her glass. His hands were almost square. His fingers were thick, the nails blunt and strong. With no alteration of tone, he added, 'You have the most beautiful breasts of any woman at this table.'

Nadia looked down before she could stop herself. The green beaded dress clung tightly to her torso. The strapless bra pushed up her cleavage. Two full curves of ivory flesh pushed up from her bodice. She flushed. 'You say that from very little knowledge.'

'I can't think of anything better to investigate. In point of fact,' he said, 'I'm a customs officer. On the river.'

'And you know all about undercover work? I'm sorry: that was obvious.' Nadia put her elbow on the table, and leaned her chin on her hand. She smiled up at him. 'I'm not usually this bad-tempered. I'm hot and bored.'

Well. Not bored. Not now.

Shannon and Corey are off looking for their chances. What about me? What if I were in bed with – *two* men like this one?

Do I dare?

The airless heat brought colour to her cheeks. She shifted in her seat. She let her stockinged leg brush against his solid thigh, through the cloth of his trousers. She wiped slick fingers on her napkin, her hands shaking, almost surprised at the suddenness of her response. *Imagine his bare body, next to mine; and a second man's hands on me . . .*

His gaze swept over the dinner guests. Under the noise of their chatter, he said, 'Formal dinners *are* boring.'

'Such a shame it isn't a Classical occasion.' She waited for an expression of puzzlement. His well-worn features flickered from surprise to quick comprehension.

'Classically Roman,' he completed. 'A Bacchanal. I don't think these people are the type.'

'Not for an orgy,' she agreed whimsically.

That body. A sense of humour. *And* education? Public school, I think. I definitely won't ask for his name. Too good to be true.

She noticed Carol at another table. 'Although one might be surprised. I remember, when I was at boarding school, we all read about the Roman Empress Messalina's competition. There wasn't one girl who didn't fantasise about trying that out.'

'A competition?'

'With a whore,' Nadia said bluntly. 'The best whore in Rome. Messalina invited her to compete for how many men they could get through in one night. Just lined them up and brought them in . . . servants, soldiers from the army, sailors off the streets.'

She looked up at him from under red lashes. She

anticipated smelling the spices on his square hands, having his strong fingers on her breasts.

'Perhaps it's the sheer number of her men that impresses me. I have very modest tastes, in reality. The height of my ambition is, oh . . .' She smiled. Her mouth was dry. She sipped red wine. *Here we go: let's just ride at the fence and take it!* Nadia continued, 'Oh . . . to take two men to bed at once, shall we say?'

He did not smile. Oh God, Nadia thought, I've shocked him. Then she noted the stillness of his expression.

The corner of his mouth lifted.

'I admire women. You're all so sensual.' The man spoke with conviction, a calm air of authority. 'All it needs is bringing out.'

'By a man, I suppose?' Nettled, Nadia spoke aloud without meaning to.

'A woman alone has desires that she won't act on.'

'Oh, but I do! The other day – no, never mind.'

In the silence, he looked away from her. A man on the far side of the table, short and young and blond, broke off from dinner conversation to acknowledge him with a nod.

'I would like to kiss the hollows behind yours ears. Your throat. Your breasts.' His voice did not move above or below a conversational tone.

Nadia slid her hand down beside her. When she put her palm on his thigh, she felt a broad leg and strong muscles. The ache in her sex began to grow. She slid her fingers towards his crotch.

He reached down and removed her hand.

'*What?*' She sighed sharply and sat back in her chair. 'Oh God. You're gay. Or you're going to say *Not here, darling* and take me back to some tacky flat.'

His long lashes lowered over his eyes. How can such a masculine-looking man have eyelashes like that? she wondered wildly. They would brush against one's skin so tantalisingly lightly . . .

'Excuse me.' His chair scraped back.

She stared after him as he marched off towards the cloakrooms. He stopped for a moment to speak to the fair-haired man who had acknowledged him. Then he walked on without looking back.

She turned to her main course, and prodded it dispiritedly with a fork.

I hate being turned down. Especially, I hate being turned down rudely. Arrogant son of a bitch!

Some minutes later his chair was moved again. She did not look up.

'Listen to me.' The man's voice was quiet. Something in it caught her attention. She moved her head very slightly to see him standing over her.

'Look down there.' His stubby finger pointed towards the bottom end of the table. Long blue velvet drapes hid the wall. The far end of the table was not occupied. 'Doors to the cloakrooms are at the far end. Go and powder your nose. When you come back, you'll find there's room to walk between the drapes and the wall. Duck down under the end of the table, where it's against the wall. Everyone will think you were bored and left.'

'Under the *table?*' Nadia's red brows lifted.

He stood beside her for a moment before sitting down. Her head was level with his waist. The sharp, elegant line of his dress trousers was broken by an unmistakable bulge at the crotch. This evidence of his calm control broken, by her, made Nadia's mouth dry. She looked up at his face, noting fine sweat just visible above his dark brows.

'You see the effect you have?' He spoke a little helplessly. Before any of the seated diners noticed, he carefully sat down. 'I'm going to drop my napkin. I'll join you under the table. Then – my friend over there will join both of us. There's an hour of speeches to come. We can do anything we like. Except make a sound.'

'I don't think I . . .'

'Go to the cloakroom.'

Nadia stood. The silk lining of her evening dress shifted over her skin. Arousal made the slight sensation a torment. She turned without looking at her companion and walked steadily down between the tables. The knowledge that he might be watching her go, knowing what he had just instructed her to do, made her wet between the legs.

In the Ladies' powder room, the yammering noise of the hall was lost. She stood alone in the heat. If only the hall were air-conditioned. If only I had drunk enough wine that I didn't have to think about this . . .

Abruptly she took the two steps back into the hall. One step sideways from the door and she was behind the drapes. It was a large gap, almost a metre wide, hot and shadowed. She trod carefully along it, not touching the curtains, not making a noise with her heels.

When she got to the end of their table, she ducked down and moved under the tablecloth. The stone floor was cool under her hands. The first trousered and stockinged legs started a few yards away.

Nadia reached back and pulled her high-heeled shoes off. Clutching them in one hand, she moved on hands and knees towards the top of the table. Voices sounded above her head in the sun-drenched dimness. I can always say I lost something, she thought. Possibly my sense of decorum. She stifled a giggle.

Avoiding the tips of shoes, she crawled to where a tiny sequinned evening bag told her her own chair stood.

A white linen napkin dropped near her face. Above her, a voice muttered an apology. What seemed like a huge male body in a dinner jacket suddenly rolled in beside her. She clutched his back, stifling a squeak.

There was just room to kneel, if she bent double. The stone was pleasantly cold under her knees. The man crouched, waiting with his head cocked. The even flow of conversation above them was not interrupted.

'Where—'

His hand was solid over her mouth. She could hardly see him in the dimness. His eyes caught the light. His pupils were wide, and dark, and urgent.

He took his hand from her mouth, and rested it on her shoulder. Nadia obeyed its pressure. She eased away from the table-strut and lay down on her back. Her shoes dropped from her hand. The smell of food and coffee and sweat was overlaid by sandalwood.

His other hand took her other shoulder. Tenderly, he cupped her flesh. He knelt beside her, pressing her down. Nadia's flesh leaped. The stone floor cooled her bare back and shoulders. She crammed her hand into her mouth to stop herself from crying out.

His face was above her for a moment. Then his head dipped. She felt the warmth of his hair pressed against the side of her face. His mouth found her ear, the hollow behind it, and his hot tongue darted into the sensitive flesh.

She shifted sideways, pressing her body up against him. Dust made grey creases on his black trousers. His body was broad, as square as his hands, his hips thick and muscled. The fly of his trousers jutted out. She dropped her fingers to his erection, feeling the heat and hardness fill her hand.

'*Mmm*—' Again, she pushed her fist into her mouth. The toe of an evening shoe grazed her shoulder. She writhed away. Frozen, she waited.

Above, conversation continued.

The ache in her pussy was a burning frustration. The need for silence frustrated her doubly. I want to tell him to have me! I want to tell him to pull my panties down and fill me!

His big body crushed against her. She rolled over on to her back. The sheer weight of his torso and hips, his thighs and shoulders, made her thrust her body up against him.

He freed his hands and lifted them to the bodice of her dress. Slowly and with exquisite care he slid the sequinned, beaded material down to her waist. He brushed his palms across her nipples, which were swelling in the strapless bra, and then eased that down. Her breasts, free, felt every whisper of warm air. Her nipples hardened instantly. He lowered his head and began to lick, chasing in spirals with his tongue over first one breast then the other, drawing close to her nipples, and then teasingly moving away.

The dress rucked up under her. It was too tight for Nadia to lift her legs and wrap them around his hips. She slid her hands around his waist, feeling the strong flat muscles of his back through his shirt. Carefully she unbuttoned his shirt. His chest was thickly hairy. She ran her fingers through it, pursued it down to the curled wisps of hair that grew thickly up the centre of his belly. She pulled his shirt out of his trousers. The thick cylindrical bulge in his pants hardened, pushing out the cloth.

With one hand to the side of his head, she drew his ear down to her mouth. She whispered, 'What about the other man – your friend?'

He rolled over on to his back and pulled her on top of him. His hot breath tingled across her cheek. 'You just let me handle this.'

Nadia lay along the warm length of his body, the

underside of the table eighteen inches above her head. She saw his pulse beating at the base of his throat. A rattle of plates brought her heart into her mouth. All conversation died.

Somewhere, towards the head of the hall, someone was striking a glass with a fork.

'My Lord, Ladies, and Gentlemen, pray silence . . .'

Oh my God, the speeches. Nadia let her weight fall on the large man beneath her. Her breasts pressed against his hairy chest, now hot and slick with sweat. He brought his head up and kissed her on the mouth, nibbling delicately at her lower lip, darting at the gap between her lips with the very tip of his tongue, until her hands came around the back of his head, and pressed him to her, and his hot writhing tongue thrust deep into her mouth.

He drew back.

Her breath heaved in her chest. Excruciatingly, she forced herself to silence. Forced herself not to ask *What the hell are you doing?*

Above them, not many tables away, a single voice began speaking.

Oh God, it's Oscar. I forgot he was making one of the speeches. Oh, poor lamb!

Laughter almost stifled her. Under the table, the man's eyes gleamed as he half sat up under her. He dropped his hands to her waist, grasped her evening dress, and eased the bottom hem up. Nadia felt her knicker-clad buttocks and hips exposed to the dusty air. The dress rucked up in a roll around her waist.

His hands slid down, fingers first, under her garter belt, under the edge of her knickers. She could not remain still. She thrust her hips down, grinding them into his crotch. His fingers pushed down into her groin, plunged into the wet hair at her crotch, and touched the entrance to her vagina. She plunged her hips down, trying to drive his fingers inside her; thick, short fingers that felt almost like a cock. She smelled his male sweat: acid, rank, enticing.

Her own sweat ran from her face, her neck; ran down over her breasts, leaving wet dusty trails. She sat back as far as the wooden surface above her allowed. His hand guided her hand to his crotch. She felt his body shudder with suppressed gasps. *That's better*. Millimetre by careful millimetre, she eased down the zip of his fly. The cloth was taut over his straining erection. She thought she heard him groan in his throat.

A thunderous burst of applause ripped the air over her head.

Nadia jumped.

Oh – the end of Oscar's speech. Yes. Of course!

Swiftly, she ripped the stranger's fly open, under cover of the noise. His erect penis sprang free. In one movement he grabbed either side of her hips and lifted her, then pulled aside the crotch of her panties, and pulled her down on to his thick, hot cock. His hands grabbed her thighs. He snagged her stockings with his caresses. The suspenders left red imprints on her white skin under the pressure. His hips thrust up, driving him deep inside her. She thrust down. She felt her body filled, pushed apart, by his amazing thickness. Mad with wanting, she plunged her body down.

His arms went around her waist. She was seized and rolled over on to her back in one dizzy second. A man's shoes flew past in her vision: she avoided them only by luck. Above them the hall was utterly silent.

His cock pushed up into her body.

I'm going to make a noise, I know I am. Oh, don't *stop!*

With a strong, unstoppable power he drew his hips

back, and thrust them forward, giving her rising pleasure. His thick cock-head slid out to the lips of her vagina, then plunged in again. Again and again: teasingly, sliding almost out of her, then the thick maleness of him thumping into her hot, aching cleft. The thick hair at his groin smeared her, wet with his sweat and her juices. His balls thudded on her anus.

Her hands reached down and seized his buttocks. Ample handfuls of flesh. As he came forward she pulled him up, up, up into her; driving in; her shoulders bouncing off the stone floor, her body pounded, inch by inch sliding up between the tables.

His cock slid out of her. Cold air hit her hot flesh with an electrifying shock. She let go of him and sat up on her elbows. She caught a look of triumph.

Bereft, aching with unfilled desire, Nadia glanced up and down the underside of the table. Legs. Shoes. Nothing else: no one pretending to drop their napkin. If that was the blond man's seat *there*, he certainly hadn't moved, hadn't made a move to join them—

I've been had. In more ways than one! Rage flashed in Nadia's eyes. She opened her mouth. Above, someone chinked a glass. An elderly, frail voice was making a speech on the far side of the hall. She tried to hush her panting breath. But I still want him, damn it!

His cool hands pushed her thighs apart. No hesitation, no nervousness. His rough hair tickled her sensitive skin and she shivered, simultaneously hot and cold. She ached to grab his cock and shove it up inside her.

His skilled tongue caressed her outer labia. She jerked, as if an electric current convulsed her. His tongue darted into her. He licked, nibbled, and began to swirl his tongue inside her. She flooded with wetness and arousal, one hand fisted and plunged into her mouth. His tongue drew close to her clit. It paused.

Then his sucking lips closed around her clitoris.

Only his hand clamped on top of hers held back her scream of pleasure. Her hips bucked. Orgasm peaked and surged through her body, flushing her skin, loosening her muscles, lifting her from the cold stone.

Nadia fell back. His arms steered her carefully to the flagstones. She looked up into his dark eyes, bright in his sweating face. She glared at him. The man lay back on his side, shirt and jacket undone, fly unzipped. His thick, blue-veined cock jutted into the air. She could not resist reaching out and stroking its silken velvet hardness.

He unceremoniously drew down her knickers, pulling her to him. The heat of his hard body warmed her from shoulders to toes. The engorged head of his cock pushed hotly against her bare belly. His hands on her buttocks crushed her to him.

Nadia felt her legs part. The table and cloth and legs forgotten, she wrapped her legs around his hips. He was hard enough that his cock needed no guidance. It slid into her wet and welcoming pussy, pushing the clenching walls apart, teasing her with its solidity.

He rolled over and began to drive into her with solid, rhythmic strokes. She drew her legs up and up. She sensed he would not stop now until he had pleasured her fully again. His thrusts penetrated deep into her core. His large, hard body bruised her breasts and ribs. Her back rubbed against the abrasive dirt on the flagstones. Her mouth wide open, she let her gasps out in almost complete silence. On and on, like a machine, thicker and harder; and she wound her fingers in his hair and clamped her eyes shut, her skin flushing hot, her sex sucking wet with the juices of this second arousal, and he arched up and pounded his come into her waiting body, and the fire between her legs flared into a searing explosion of pleasure so intense it was almost pain.

Nadia sprawled on her back on the floor.

Outside the table, a more prolonged burst of applause sounded.

'What happened to your "friend"?' Nadia demanded in a whisper. 'You didn't talk to that man about this. You lied! You didn't even *mention* this to anyone else! I suggested *two* men!'

'There aren't two men like me,' he said simply. Sprawled back on buttocks and elbows in the dim light, he looked both rumpled and annoyingly calm.

'You enjoyed it, didn't you?' He smiled in the dimness. 'Sweet woman. It's pretty obvious you just need one man who can bring you out of yourself.'

'I need *what?*'

The applause died away to silence.

Her hands clenched into fists.

Infuriated by his calm control, Nadia glared. She wanted to shout and she wanted to kick him and neither was possible. Do I *really* mind if I'm found here? Wouldn't it be worth it? Just to slap his arrogant face?

'We must do this again sometime.' He leaned over and made as if to hold up the edge of the snowy linen tablecloth.

Nadia grabbed his hand.

He put his mouth against her ear. 'And you told me you were a dare-devil.'

Nadia turned her back on him. It was not easy, she had to push under and past his sweat-soaked body.

Half-naked, her shoes in her hands, she crawled with what she hoped was dignity back towards the blue velvet drapes and the exit to the Ladies' powder room.

'What an arsehole!' Corey flared up.

Shannon was laughing. 'That's sweet! Well, no. You know what I mean. Not sweet, exactly. More . . .'

'Irritating,' Nadia completed. She looked demurely under her lashes at her younger friends. 'He did do it so well. It's just that I want to hit him.'

Corey pulled a tendril of black hair forward. It was just long enough for her to suck one end. 'I'd kick him in the bollocks!'

'If he hadn't been so arrogant, I would have enjoyed it immensely.' Nadia stopped, and corrected herself. 'I did enjoy *it*. I would have enjoyed *him*, without wanting to kick him in the – er – bollocks. Regrettably, I didn't acquire his name or telephone number. I thought too much of a good thing was enough. Now,' she said, 'what do we do? Do we accept Michael's verdict? That Corey is the winner?'

There was a moment's silence.

'Oh, what does he know?' Corey leaned her elbows on the supper table. 'We know each other best, after all, don't we? Better than he does. It isn't about 'telling good stories'. It's about *fucking!*'

Shannon smiled affectionately at the girl. The top two buttons of Shannon's silk blouse were open again; the lower one was actually missing. She tugged them together absentmindedly. 'If we're ever going to get a proper winner, let's go back to different dares. Half the fun is tailoring them to each person.'

'I'm not convinced Shannon should have lost, either,' Corey added, with a careless generosity that made Nadia smile. 'Technically I didn't have sex with two guys either, I was there while sex was being had. I wasn't the one in the middle. And I think yours was dead good, Nadia, even if it wasn't a proper dare. I don't think you *can* dare yourself.'

'It's got me through life so far,' Nadia said mildly. 'Shannon?'

The woman pushed her fingers through her curly brown hair. Beyond her, through the window, heat-lightning flickered on the horizon. Ten o'clock and the sunset sky scarcely dark yet. 'The trouble is, it's so difficult to judge, because it's so difficult to know.'

'Yeah. *We* might think Edward and James weren't hunks at all,' Corey confirmed.

She began suddenly to smile.

Nadia sat up, keeping her gaze on Corey, feeling the young woman's contagious excitement. 'But it's been so difficult to get real proof. What do you suggest?'

'I know exactly what we should get. *Photographic proof!*'

Nadia stared.

Corey's young face was alight. 'I've just realized. *I* could develop the films. There wouldn't be any trouble about that, I can do it at home. That's a challenge – not only do you have to take your dare, you have to bring back photographic proof. That'll sort out the winners from the losers!'

Shannon Garrett let out a breath. 'That would be a challenge. How on earth could . . .'

'And I tell you what. As soon as we get a proper winner – they get to choose how we spend William Jenson's five thousands pounds.'

Chapter Seven

NADIA LOOKED CAREFULLY at Corey's flushed face. There was something both frantic and oddly absent-minded about her excitement.

Just as Nadia was forming the thought, Shannon asked, 'Corey, is everything OK? There isn't something bothering you?'

'Not about this,' the girl assured them carelessly. 'Hey, one of you will have to set me a dare, too, so that I get a chance to compete. Well? Shall we do it?'

'I suppose we must.' Nadia laughed helplessly. 'How can we refuse? It does answer the question about the five thousand pounds. But taking *photographs!*'

'You can do it! Make mine a really good dare. Don't go away!' The black-haired girl sprang to her feet and seized her car keys from among a heap of commemorative medallions on a side table. 'Make coffee or something. I'll be back in ten minutes!'

Nadia shook her head. 'Hopeless girl! Where are you going?'

'To get my spare camera!' Corey popped her head back around the flat's front door. 'One of you will need to borrow it. I've already thought of the next dares I'm going to set.'

The two women were left alone in a companionable silence.

Nadia moved to the big leather armchair by the stuffed alligator and curled up comfortably. A cooler breeze feathered her skin. A handful of fat rain drops plummeted out of the darkening sky, splashing back from the white-painted window-sill. She let the smell of rain and dust permeate. The only light inside the high room came from the last two dinner candles.

She heard Shannon get up. The other woman went off into the kitchen. Nadia heard her making coffee, finding where everything was with the ease of long familiarity. She had lived here as long as Shannon had known her.

The rattle of the rain increased. Spray bounced in, soaking a row of commemoration pewter pots. Nadia got up out of the armchair and went to lower the window. She left a six inch gap at the bottom, for air.

'I put the percolator on, there's enough for three.' Shannon's hand put a coffee mug into the narrow space on the junk-filled side table that could accommodate it. The younger woman went to stand in front of the window, cradling her mug between her palms. Nadia bent her head and inhaled the coffee smell.

'She's riding that bike in the rain again,' Shannon said.

Nadia smoothed a curl of red hair back behind her ear. 'Do you know, that's just what I was thinking.'

'Do you ever hear from her mother these days?'

'Oh, Maria writes twice a year. The last I heard, she and John were becoming very prosperous in Brazil. She's much happier back at home there than she ever was in London. She always tells me to keep an eye on her "little Corazon".'

'That's Spanish, isn't it?'

'I imagine so. Maria was a Ramirez before she married John Black, or so Oscar used to tell me.' Nadia chuckled. 'Maria makes me feel so old, sometimes! I feel much more as though I were Corey's age.'

The other woman muttered, 'Corey makes me feel as if I were an inexperienced fifteen-year-old. She always did, even when she was twelve!'

Rain drummed ferociously on the dark glass. Nadia sipped her coffee. She smiled up at the woman by the window.

'I think, if we're inventive, we can come up with a dare even Corey will regard as a challenge.'

Corey gave them two carelessly scrawled notes. They gave her a slip of paper, written by Shannon, and signed by them both.

'I have to open the shop *some* days,' was Nadia's firm farewell. 'I do have a living to earn. Let's meet Sunday week.'

Shannon drove home and parked the Rover in the garage block. She walked back around to her house through warm night rain. The moisture clung to her hair, dampened her face.

She stood for a second outside her terraced house.

Corey's folded note was in her jacket pocket. She had deliberately not read it. She paused under the orange glow of the street lights.

Shall I . . .?

She briskly got out her keys and let herself in.

Her bedroom was warm, even with the windows open. Shannon lay down naked on top of the sheet. Her eyes went to the shadowed shape that was her jacket, hung over the back of her chair. To put the light on, to read whatever was written there: it would be so easy.

Shannon's hand strayed over her thigh and between her legs.

It could be anything. Her fingers moved fast, then slow, then fast again. The dim light from the street lamp glimmered on her breasts and thighs. *Absolutely anything. . .*

Do I dare?

Her breathing quickened. A little later, her lips curved in a smile of anticipation, she fell asleep in the hot summer night.

Nadia Kay remained sitting in the big armchair in her living-room. The candles melted down to stubs. Rain spattered the windows. Soft yellow light shone on the walls, crowded with posters and prints, and the boxes of old magazines.

Corey knows me very well. Too well!

She looked down at the scrawled note. Corey's handwriting was extremely flamboyant. Nadia thought, yes, she might well end that one with an exclamation mark! It deserves it.

Do I *quite* dare. . .?

Corey pulled the bike up halfway around the North Circular. She stopped on a garage forecourt, under the lights, and took off her gloves and helmet to read Shannon's neat handwriting again.

We dare you to have sex with someone in a supermarket.

Corey's black eyebrows went up. In a *supermarket?*

That's all very well for them to say! Pick up some guy in a supermarket, no problem. I've watched Friday night cruising by the pasta shells. But doing *sex* in a supermarket – and taking a photograph – the question is, *how?*

Three days later she had a grand total of two refusals, four looks of complete incomprehension, and a regretful smile from a gay till assistant.

I need a new approach, she decided.

Corey pushed the shopping trolley ahead of her down the supermarket aisle. There were fewer shoppers around now, on a week-day, with only quarter of an hour to go before closing. The overhead lights had been dimmed in the fresh bread and patisserie counter area. Everywhere else was still bright.

She checked the position of the security guards.

A tall, lean man stood by the revolving door exit. He wore a smart grey uniform. Dark hair. Glasses. Corey thought, Yeah, that one's good.

The second security guard was burly and fair-haired, and probably a year younger than Corey. He caught her eye. An intelligent, sharp face. She ignored him and continued on down the aisle.

It's no good trying to just look suspicious. I have to be suspicious.

She re-ran her fantasy in her head: *I know I've been shoplifting, sir, but if you let me go, I'll be really nice to you* . . . A pulse of warmth flickered between her legs.

Corey looked at the crowded shelves. She would need to take some small item, to make it convincing. Something not very expensive.

Oh, damn! I don't have pockets.

She came to a dead halt as she turned to go up the neighbouring aisle, and looked down at herself. The June evening was hot. She was wearing black jeans and a scoop-necked T-shirt, and sandals. The trolley so far contained a can of beans and her minuscule shoulder-bag. She had forgotten to bring even a light jacket.

The chatter of shoppers diminished, and she heard

the clatter of the till drawers cease. The last announcement of the store closing sounded over the tannoy. Almost too late to do anything now.

In desperation she wheeled the trolley towards the bakery section where the lights were lowered. The department closed earlier than the others, being out of fresh bread.

Once there, she leaned her arms forward on the rail of her trolley and stared around desperately.

This isn't going to work.

Wait a minute . . .

She remembered once reading an article, probably in *Femme*, about shoplifters who wore baggy knickers, specially designed to hide small articles under their clothing. That'll have to do, Corey thought. I'll improvise. She glanced around. The tannoy binged again. *'This store is now closed. Will all customers please make their way to the nearest till.'* In a panic, she looked at the shelf nearest to her. She was standing by the cool cupboards. The nearest display was one of hard-shelled meringues. The labels alternately said 'jam-filled' or 'cream-filled'.

Well, they're small, she thought. Quickly she reached out and took a cool, smooth ovoid between her fingers. With her other hand, she pulled the waistband of her jeans open. She realised as she slid the meringue past her belt that she had caught the waistband of her lace knickers, too. The hard-shelled meringue slid down inside her knickers and came to rest just below the curve of her stomach. It was cold against her bare flesh. She looked down. The cloth was loose enough that nothing was visible.

Frantic, Corey looked up and down the aisle. No one. No security guard.

She heard the revolving doors at the front of the store stop moving. Staff called to each other. The doors were locked, grills rattling down. One security guard called a good-night – the older or the younger? No way to tell. Corey nodded in satisfaction. Now to hide until everyone except the last security guard had left.

The cool meringue shell shifted in her jeans as she began to push her trolley. It wasn't enough, she decided. It didn't show. He might just think she was a lost customer, and show her out of the door.

Quickly Corey reached out and picked up two more meringues, and slid them under her waistband, down her knickers. They lodged next to the first. Just visible as a bulge.

Walking carefully, she pushed her trolley quietly a few feet further into the bakery department, where the lights were lowest. She paused by the refrigerated compartments. The filled meringues were cold and surprisingly heavy, pulling the fabric of her jeans and pants down. Perhaps they still weren't enough. Something else, small?

She reached out and picked up one of the cakes. A cream-filled éclair. Not practical, she thought. No—

'Can I help you, miss?' A deep male voice boomed in her ear.

In a complete panic, Corey forgot that she was planning to be discovered. She had her back to the man. Instantly she pulled the neck of her T-shirt forward, popped the cream éclair down her ample cleavage, and let the cloth spring back to conceal it.

'I, er—' she looked over her shoulder, her hands now innocently gripping the handle of the supermarket trolley. With relief, she remembered that she needed to look guilty for her plan to work.

It was the fair-haired guard. Maybe a year or two younger than her. Taller. He folded his arms and looked down at her. He had a sharp face, and long-lashed pale eyes. The top button of his uniform collar was undone, and a curl of gold hair poked out between his shirt buttons. He said softly, 'What have we here, then . . .'

Corey shrugged, and gave a sickly grin. 'I can explain.'

'I've been watching you. Shoplifting is a crime, miss,' he said. There was a glint in his eyes. Corey wondered if she ought to confess all of it, the dare included. I don't want to *actually* get arrested! she realised.

The young security man padded past her on silent feet. She had no idea how so big a man moved so quietly. The glint was still in his eyes. A grin joined it. He faced her, putting both hands on the far end of her trolley, and leaned forward, so that they were almost face to face.

Corey was dry-mouthed. Without meaning to, she denied it. 'I'm not a shoplifter!'

'Not even a little bit?' His voice sounded cynical now, teasing. Corey thought, this is just the kind of boy who would take up my bargain – but I'm not so sure I want him to.

'Not at all,' she said firmly, brazening it out. 'I just stayed in the shop too long.'

He laughed. His hands clenched on the wire trolley. 'That right, miss? Then if I searched you, I wouldn't find any evidence, would I?'

The cool, heavy meringues rubbed against the soft skin of her belly as she straightened up defiantly. The éclair inside her shirt slipped down a fraction. She was sweating: it was slick against her skin. Her brain raced. If only she had been innocent, she would have demanded to be taken to the store manager's office. As it was . . .

'You won't find anything!' she snapped, lying weakly.

His pale eyes shone as he smiled at her. 'I think I will.'

The shopping trolley shifted under her hands. He moved before she realised it. She had no chance of stopping him. He grasped his end of the shopping trolley and jerked it sharply away from him, towards Corey. Her hands clenched on the rail too late. The hard metal mesh of the trolley smacked into her belly.

There was a soft but audible crunch.

She felt the shells of the meringues in her pants smash. Cold, sticky cream shot across her stomach. Jam-filling drenched her crotch, and slid down her thighs. The trolley moved back an inch. Broken meringue shell crunched in her knickers, plastered across her belly.

'Oh!' Corey gasped. She stood stiff-legged, her face flaming. She looked down.

A dark patch spread on the outside of the crotch of her black jeans. As she watched, a trickle of jam and cream ran out of her jeans leg, down her ankle, and pooled on the floor.

The big young man smiled wolfishly. 'That's evidence of shoplifting, miss – now you can't put them back on the shelves and say it never happened.'

'*Oh!*' Almost speechless, Corey gritted her teeth and tugged the front of her jeans away from her body. Her fingers slipped on the slimy cloth. The material smacked wetly back against her skin. 'How *dare* you!'

He drew himself up, shoulders straightening. With strong and deliberate movements he put the trolley aside and stepped closer. 'And I don't think that's all, is it? You might as well confess and get it over with.'

She didn't know what to say or do. She blurted, 'I didn't take anything else!'

He was so close to her now that she had to crane her neck to look up at him. His grey uniform jacket concealed a strong, fast body.

In one swift movement he put the palm of his hand flat on her T-shirt, above her cleavage, made a fist of his other hand, and brought it down on top of the first hand with a smart smack.

'No!' she cried out, too late.

The cream-filled éclair smashed inside her shirt. It was cold, being from the cooler cupboard display. Icy-cold cream squirted across her breasts, down the cleft between them, and pushed its way into her bra. His hands kneaded her breasts through the cloth, spreading the sticky cream.

'See,' he said smugly.

He's going to have me arrested, Corey thought in abject humiliation. He's going to take me to the manager's office and the police station *like this*. I'll die!

With that thought came a twinge of arousal. She studied the look in his eye. His face was shadowed now the shop lights were down. Impossible really to read his expression. But, for a security guard, he was taking a long time to sound the alarm . . .

Maybe William Jenson knew what he was saying, Corey reflected. Maybe he did teach me something about what I like done to me. Inside her bra, her cream-smeared nipples were standing up hard as two little pebbles. She began to look at the strong young man with confidence.

'Takes a thief to catch a thief,' she said.

'What?'

'How many other poor little bimbos have you tried this on with?'

The mask of cynicism slipped for a moment. Hurriedly, the young man muttered, 'No, you're wrong, I've always wanted to, but I never—'

Corey's grin became triumphant.

'Well,' she said softly, 'that doesn't surprise me. Because you forgot the one thing you're going to find impossible to explain away.'

He took her arm, preparing to lead her away, turning as he did so. 'What's that?'

She was already moving while he was speaking, and it caught him off-guard. With one hand she reached out to the cold cabinet and grabbed an aerosol can of cream, thumbing off the plastic top. Her other hand seized his leather belt and pulled the back of his uniform trousers, with their knife-edge creases, open. She plunged the nozzle of the can down the seat of his trousers and jammed her thumb on the button.

'*You little cow!*' His voice shot up an octave.

Both his hands behind him, he grabbed at her wrists, tugging, wrestling, trying desperately to pull her hands away. Corey laughed excitedly. Her fingers were locked into the back of his leather belt. Her hands were slippery now, as the cream pumped into his boxer shorts. She kept her grip.

At last the can fizzled and ran empty.

Corey pried her hands away.

She looked up at the blond security man. His jaw had dropped. He gazed at her, open-mouthed.

'You can't do that!' The waistband of his trousers was smeared with white cream. Nothing else was visible but a huge wet bulge in the seat of his pants. Corey gently reached out, cupped her hands under it, and squashed upwards. He shut his eyes in anguish.

'Explain *that* to your manager,' she exclaimed with satisfaction.

She wiped her sticky hand across his fly. Under her palm, she felt his cock twitch through the slimy material.

She replaced her hand on the stiff bulge of cream in his trousers, pushed it down between his straddled legs, and then put her hands on the outside of his muscular thighs. Firmly, she shut his legs together.

There was an audible squelch.

Still resting her palm against his cock, she reached into the cool cabinet and drew out a heavy cream flan.

'You wouldn't dare,' he husked. When she looked up, the light was back in his eyes. Anticipation. Defiance.

'I'm your nightmare come true, sonny.' She pushed the cream pie right into his face. Under her hand, his cock swelled and lengthened. He lifted his hands to scoop the soft, sticky mess away.

'Come with me – miss.' His index finger hooked over the front of her jeans and tugged sharply. The wet material slid snugly up into the cleft of her buttocks. Denim, sticky with cream, was yanked up between her swelling labia. With no choice, she submitted to the pressure and walked forward. Her knickers clung to her skin inside her jeans, cloth sliding slimily across her stomach. A warmth grew in her pussy, somewhere between power and humiliation.

He drew her down the aisle between the freezers and the bakery department. Corey looked at the meringue cases, the sticky buns, the cream cakes. 'You wouldn't dare. I'll tell.'

'If I can't tell, you certainly can't.' Both his hands dropped to her waist. He spun her around so she faced away from the counter.

She felt his fingers swiftly yank her fly buttons undone. He pulled her jeans down to her knees. Corey opened her mouth to protest. She felt his strong young hands seize her either side of her waist and lift.

Her feet left the floor. She yelped. She had a brief glimpse of his grin as he whirled her around, paused for a second, and then sat her squarely down on the counter – in the middle of a huge chocolate gateau. There was a squelch. Chocolate icing and cream filling shot up between her thighs. Sticky cream filled her vagina. His hands did not loosen their grip, but pushed her down into the chilly mess.

Corey squirmed helplessly. Still holding her, he bent his head and began to nuzzle between her thighs. His tongue found her clit. She squirmed deeper into the cold, smooth, sensual mess. She found herself wriggling to smear the gateau further over her buttocks and thighs. The lacy material of her frilled knickers grew sopping wet.

At last he stepped back, letting her go. His smeared face was dazzled.

She eased herself gingerly, stickily, down from the counter. Her jeans entangled her knees. She tugged them up as far as they would go, the wet denim clinging to her skin. The tactile sensation of slipperiness aroused her. Her sex was so swollen with lust that she could hardly walk. Faltering, she moved to stand in front of him.

He reached a big hand out, caressing her cream-smeared breast through the wet cloth of her T-shirt. His eyes met hers in wonder. 'My God. I *never* thought I'd get to do this. I want you. Now!'

'There's something you're going to get first.' Corey smiled. 'Or should I say, do first.' She pointed at the cold compartment. 'Fill your pants.'

Even in the shadowed supermarket gloom, she saw his face change. 'No,' he whispered.

Corey stroked the back of her hand up the front of his trousers. He was strainingly erect. She tapped the radio hanging on his belt. 'You wouldn't want me to call the rest of the staff, would you? Maybe I don't care. Maybe I think it'd be worth it, to see your face. Now do what I tell you. I'll say when it's enough.'

He reached out to the boxes with his hands trembling, took a meringue, and put it down the front of his damp uniform trousers. He looked anxiously at

Corey. Smiling, she shook her head.

The blond man hefted three meringues in his big hand, and carefully tucked them down his trousers. Then he shrugged, took down a carton, and emptied that down his pants. Corey saw the heavy, cream-filled ovoids bagging out the crotch of his uniform. She said, 'And again, I think . . .'

He gave her one beseeching look. She was adamant. One by one, he pushed five fragile shells down his trousers, until he paused with the last meringue in his hand.

'Might as well be hung for a sheep as a lamb,' he grinned. Corey felt him tug the front of her T-shirt forward and tuck the meringue down between her breasts. Her skin was hot, flushed: her nipples hard in anticipation. He put his palm on her shirt and slowly and deliberately pushed. There was a minute of aching expectation. The meringue suddenly popped. Her eyes shot open wide. A rush of cold cream squished down her breasts and belly. Cream slid smoothly down over her flushed, aroused skin.

She put his hands on her breasts and pressed them hard against her. While he stood like that, she dropped her hands, flattened her palms, and smacked them both firmly across his belly. She felt the meringues crush under her hands. His eyes shut. He shuddered. His hard cock pushed at her hands through the cream-wet cloth.

'That feels fantastic. I wouldn't have dared . . .' He opened his eyes. His face was flushed. He gazed down at her, worriedly. 'We shouldn't be doing this, should we?'

She slid her hands down his trousers to his crotch, then brought one hand up sharply between his legs. His hard-on was by now rock-solid.

'Games are fun,' she said. And she smiled wickedly.

'Aren't they?'

Shame-faced, he grinned. Corey hooked her ankle behind the young man's leg and yanked. She felt him give way to the movement, falling back on the floor. She measured her length along his body, belly to belly. The smashed meringues inside his pants, between them, smeared her crotch too. She wrenched at the zip of his trousers. She stopped, astride. She stood and pulled her T-shirt off, and bent to pull down her jeans, but by the time he had stripped off his uniform jacket and shirt together, and caught hold of the cuffs of her jeans, pushed her down, and pulled them off in one swift movement. They lay slick flesh to slick flesh, in the running juices of food. She instantly mounted his stiff cock, plunging it deep into her ready sex, crying out with anguish and pleasure together, and came twice before his rapid, frantic strokes climaxed in a first flood of seed.

Some minutes later he prowled off barefoot and stark naked to the wine department. When he came back, he knelt beside her. Corey's flesh jerked as cold liquid fizzed over her breasts and stomach, and ran down between her legs.

'It's champagne,' he whispered. 'I'm washing you in champagne.'

His tongue rasped from the sticky hair around her sex, up over the curve of her belly, dipped into her navel, licked up across her breasts, and finished with a deep, champagne-tasting kiss.

Corey sat up with her back to the freezer compartment. As he knelt up before she, she scooped at random and brought out two handfuls of chocolate cream. She held his eye for a second. Then she pressed both hands over his hard, hot cock.

'Oh, shit!' he groaned.

'Don't worry.' The smell of chocolate and champagne

invaded her senses. Corey ran her fingers through his matted hair and took hold of his cock. She lay down beside him. 'I'll clean you up,' she said, and began to lick, delicately and raspingly.

'That's good . . . ' his voice purred deceptively. She felt his body move. Then:

'Oh!' she squealed. Something freezing cold and sticky slammed up between her legs. Her thighs clamped together on his hand, and on an ice-cream gateau from the fridge.

'Fair exchange,' he offered, and bent his head to mouth at the freezing ice-cream now running over her hot labia, sucking her, his tongue chasing into the folds of her flesh.

Not long before the early summer dawn she got up and padded barefoot to the abandoned shopping trolley. She reached into her shoulder-bag.

'You might want to turn your head away,' Corey said.

He asked, 'Why?'

Corey held up the tiny camera in her palm. 'You wouldn't want to be recognised, I don't suppose.'

The young security guard reached into the freezer. His hand came out holding a chocolate cheesecake, soft, half-defrosted. 'You hide my face,' he invited.

There was a squelch. The camera's flash fired twice.

Chapter Eight

THE SUMMER'S HOT sun burned through the office windows. Even with the slatted blinds drawn, it was hot and airless. Shannon walked through the open-plan office, between the grey work-station partitions, to her own room. Small, it might be. Shelved from floor to ceiling and spilling back issues of *Femme* everywhere it also might be. But it's mine, she thought as she closed the door. And God knows I worked hard enough to get it!

She threw her briefcase down on the desk. Her large window slid out the statutory two inches. Petrol-smelling air leaked in from the Strand. Air-conditioning, what's that? she thought, and sat down with a thud. You'd think being owned by an American firm would make some difference . . .

And this isn't what I'm really thinking about.

'Coffee?' Arabella put her head round the office door.

'Oh – no thanks.' She sighed. 'Give me half an hour to shift some of this stuff, and then I'll have some iced tea, if there's any left. Is Jane coming in for her appointment at ten-thirty?'

Her assistant nodded and left.

Shannon knew she had twenty minutes undisturbed at the outside. She picked up the phone and dialled an outside line.

It rang for almost two minutes. Then:

'Mmrh? Whassat?'

'Corey, it's me. Shannon.'

'Um.' There was a pause, in which Shannon could all but see the black-haired girl roll over on her futon and knuckle sleep out of her eyes. Corey's voice sharpened. 'Fuck me, is that the *time*? I'm supposed to be in Hammersmith!'

Shannon sat forward in her chair. She could see nothing through her room's glass walls but heads bent over IBM work-stations. 'Corey . . .'

There was a pause.

'I know what you're going to say.' Corey's voice rode over Shannon's as she finally tried to get out another sentence. She was bright, confident. Shannon thought, She's done her dare. She's actually done it . . .

'Shannon, I'm just going to say one thing. Don't take the dare – *if* you can say you've never fantasised about it. Never. Not even once. OK? Otherwise, believe me, I dare you!'

There was a longer pause.

Shannon heard her own voice crackle down the line. 'Do you know Nadia as well as you know me?'

'I don't know. Do I? Gotta go!' Her phone clicked down in its cradle.

Shannon sat holding the phone until it buzzed its long complaint.

On Saturday morning Shannon stood, undecided, on Waterloo Station concourse.

The sun glittered in through glass windows from a sky tending towards the overcast. Shannon straightened her shoulders. The straps of her bikini top tightened over her collar-bones. She wore a loose shirt and a flowing Indian skirt over the top of her bikini, and a pair of thonged sandals. She carried a light shoulder-bag that held a few beach things and a book, a rolled-up towel and a phone. And a camera.

Her eyes searched the departures board for trains to the coast.

There's always the chance, she mused, that the woman who wrote that article didn't know what she was talking about. Did we publish it? Oh, that's right, it'll be in the August issue.

In which case, it's just as well I'm going before the place gets popular.

Shannon read a book from the time when the train departed until the time some hours later when it drew into the coastal station. She closed the book with no knowledge of what she had been reading. As she put the book away in her bag and queued to leave the train, she thought, No, I can't say I *never* fantasised about it. Damn you, Corey, you brat!

Here, away from London, the air smelled clean. A brilliant sun was hazed whitely over from time to time, and a brisk wind blew. It made the streets comfortably rather than unbearably hot. Shannon paused on her walk from the station and bought herself a broad-brimmed sun hat. She adjusted her sunglasses, looking at the brilliance of the seaside town's streets, thronged with tourists and children eating ice-cream.

It's a bit crowded. Hell, it's a lot crowded.

Oh well, the article did say you had to walk quite a way . . .

She found the sign-posted footpath from the promenade and gratefully left the thronging families behind.

A silence fell amazingly quickly. She climbed up the footpath, away from the town. Traffic noise died. A thin, high song rang out in the blue above her. She dredged the bird's name from childhood memories: a skylark. Its song was drowned out, as she walked further on, by the yelping of gulls.

The rough track climbed more steeply, until it came out on to a grassy plateau. Shannon panted. She stopped and took her shoes off, carrying them in her hand. She dug her toes into the cool grass. A muscle-tension she had been unaware of left her. Whether anything happens or not, she thought, I'm glad I came.

Shannon walked slowly on. Something glittered in front of her. She crested the shallow slope. The sea, sunlit and brilliant, stretched away to the south. The scent of salt was strong. Gulls wheeled and cried. Ahead of her, the path dropped in steep curves down a bank, almost a cliff. It ran into a secluded bay. Cliffs cut the bay off from all sides, except where silver sand ran down to the sea.

Shannon drew a breath. A few tiny figures ran among the foam. Swimmers' heads bobbed like dark pinheads. She could not tell from this distance whether they were all women.

She realised she had been standing still for several minutes.

The sun began to burn her shoulders. She walked on, to where the path dipped over the cliff-edge. She could only watch where she put her feet, then, unable to spare any attention for anything else. The wind whisked her skirts. She grabbed her hat with one hand. The strap of her bag cut into her shoulder.

The breeze died. A warm air brushed her face. Her bare feet stood on the edge of sand. Shannon lifted her head and realised she was down in the secluded cove. The packed sand here was warm and slightly damp under her toes. Groups of people in brightly-coloured swimsuits and bikinis ran close to the water-line, laughing, their voices echoing back from the cliffs above.

One of the women in a closer group waved a hand and called, 'Hi! That water's *cold!*'

'Um, I don't think I'll swim yet. Thanks.' Hastily, Shannon moved away. She walked rapidly along the beach, or as rapidly as the sand would permit. 'Idiot!' she muttered to herself. I can turn around right now and go home if I want to.

But I don't want to.

She found a stretch of sand not far from the bottom of the cliffs. The cliffs did not go straight up here. There had obviously been a landslip at some time in the past. The hillocks of earth had long ago become overgrown by long grass and waving wild flowers. Bees buzzed in the heat. Shannon stretched out her towel. She knelt on it and took off her shirt, and then slipped her skirt down over her hips. The thin material of her blue and gold bikini clung to her stomach and hips, and enclosed her breasts tautly. Whether it was the hot sensual afternoon or some other reason, she felt aroused.

She remained kneeling on her towel in the sun. Some yards away, at the shoreline, two young women walked hand in hand in the spreading fans of water. One slipped her arm unselfconsciously around the other's waist. Her hand slid down to cup her companion's bikini-clad buttock.

I guess the article was right, Shannon reflected.

She took her book out of her bag and opened it. She lay down with it in front of her. The soft sand gave slightly under her thighs and hips. When she removed her sunglasses the light was too bright. She put them back, watching the beach from behind their security.

Women of all ages sat in groups on the sand, or

played with frisbees, or swam. She let her eye linger. There were a few very young male children, but no men.

Not far away, a woman on her own was sunbathing on a towel. She looked about twenty-three. Her hair was long, black, and fell in ringlets. Shannon watched the gentle rise and and fall of her ribcage. She thought, a man would watch those breasts swelling out of that bikini-top, with their faint hint of a tan.

The woman stirred. She rolled over on to her front. Shannon caught sight of a strong-featured face, and eyes squinting shut against the sun. Then the young woman was lying face down. Her long legs were freckled with sand that dried from ochre to white on her skin. A man would look at that round bottom, split by an emerald-coloured thong. A man would feel . . . what?

Shannon became aware of warmth between her legs.

She sat up and reached for the sun-block in her bag. The plastic canister felt cool. She squirted the pale liquid into her palm and smoothed it up her arms and shoulders. Her hands slid over the tops of her breasts. She refilled her palm and smoothed the sun-block over her stomach; over her thighs and calves.

'Do your back if you want?'

Shannon's head jerked up. She smiled in confusion. The young woman with the ringlets was standing above her. The white sunlight shone fiercely on her flat stomach, pale thighs, and emerald-green bikini. Shannon looked up. The young woman's mouth was too big for beauty, and her dark eyebrows too thick. Her eyes were half hooded against the sun, but when Shannon made eye-contact, there was a long, level stare coming back at her. Shannon stopped smiling.

'You've got such fair skin, you'll burn,' Shannon said. 'How about if I do you first? Then you can do me.

Why don't you bring your towel over here?'

'Sure.' The young woman moved back towards it on long legs. Over her shoulder, she said, 'I'm Laura.'

'Elaine.'

'Hi, Elaine.' The towel flopped into the sand. The woman knelt down on it and plunged forward as if she were diving. She sprawled on her stomach on the sun-warmed material. 'You're right, I'm starting to burn, I'm sore.'

'Don't worry.' Shannon picked up the sun-block. 'I'll fix it.'

The breeze from the sea feathered the fine hairs on her arms. It blew her hair into her face. She squirted a generous quantity of sun-block into her palm. For a moment she hesitated. Then she reached down and rubbed her palm across the middle of the young woman's back, below black flowing hair.

Her hand encountered warm, soft skin that shivered at her touch and then quieted. Laura said nothing. She stroked the liquid across Laura's shoulder-blades, under the thong of her bikini top. Shannon reached down and brushed the woman's hair forwards. Then she stroked her hand across the tops of the woman's shoulders. The cool liquid sank into her fine-downed skin.

Shannon leaned back. This time she rubbed sun-block on both her palms. Then she leaned forward and massaged the young woman's foot. Gradually she worked her way up the calf. She squirted liquid on her hands and found them trembling. Suddenly unnerved, she began on the woman's other foot. She worked the liquid into the firm warm flesh, stroking it up towards the woman's knees.

How can I be sure that . . .?

I suppose I'm about to find out.

Shannon poured a little liquid into the palm of one

hand and carefully tipped it on to the back of Laura's right thigh. The thigh twitched, like a pony when a fly lands on it. As Shannon's hands pressed into the soft, cool flesh, Laura stilled. Shannon pushed her thumbs into the firm warmness, trailed her fingers back down the outside of Laura's leg without breaking contact, she pushed her fingers back up the thigh, up to the cleft where the woman's taut buttock jutted up. She smeared sun-block on to the outside curve of Laura's buttock, which was not covered by the emerald bikini.

Shannon found her hands automatically reach out to pull the knotted thong undone. She stopped. To give just one tug, see the flimsy material fall away . . .

She re-charged her hands with sun-block and began to massage Laura's other thigh, pushing the flesh up, smearing sun-block over the outer curve of that buttock. Her fingers moved up to the indentation where Laura's backbone dipped under the bikini pants. By an effort of will Shannon made her hands move up, up towards the underside of the woman's sharply-jutting shoulder-blades. Shannon's sex throbbed once, warmly. She flattened her palms on the girl's warm back.

'Here, I'll help.' Laura's hand snaked up behind her own back. She grabbed the string of her bikini top and pulled. The knot fell undone. Her hand went back down to pillow her cheek. The emerald green bikini top fell flat on the towel. Shannon saw the firm bare curves where Laura's breasts were squashed under her body.

Trembling, she slid her greasy hands around the young woman's torso. She dipped her fingers down, so far down, not quite daring to touch where the breasts began. With both palms flat, she caressed down to Laura's firm waist.

Shannon felt the crotch of her bikini pants growing

damp. Her breathing quickened. She sat back on her heels. Her nipples began to harden under her bikini top. With a momentary loss of nerve, Shannon thought, *What if she sees!*

I want her to. I really want her to.

'I'll do you now, if you like.' Laura's voice was lazy, deep and dark. She sat up. Creases from the towel were imprinted on the skin of her bare breasts. 'Lie down on your back.'

Shannon did not remove her sunglasses. She eased herself down on her back under the glistening sky. Wind blew a scurry of sand across the towels. Happy voices called from far off: the tide was going out.

Shannon shut her eyes. She felt warmth and moving air. Smells of salt, ozone and sweat permeated her senses. She waited.

A cool, cream-slick hand touched her foot. As Shannon relaxed back, Laura's fingers slid up the outsides of her calves, paused, and sank back down. Up. Down. Rhythmic strokes, smoothing the liquid over her hot skin, almost massaging it in. The firm hands slid up again to her other knee. Shannon lifted her knee slightly. The fingers slid in to the soft hollow behind her knee and out again. The procedure was repeated with Shannon's other knee. Then the hands removed themselves.

It was hardly a second until Shannon felt herself touched again. Flat palms curved around her thighs above her knee. Laura's hands pushed firmly upwards, massaging the muscle, covering Shannon's already-greasy skin in more sun-block. The sensual movement drove her wild. The warmth in her sex was becoming a hot fire of arousal. She moved, bit back a moan.

The hands massaged her other thigh, sliding up into the sensitive skin around her groin, back away, then up again. Shannon tried to keep her hips from lifting. She kept her eyes closed.

Laura's hands left her.

There was a longer pause than normal. Shannon opened her eyes. The young woman had her head bent over the sun-block container. She wore only her emerald bikini bottom. Her breasts were small but full, the nipples a very pale pink. The pressure-marks of the towel had almost vanished now.

Laura straightened. Shannon hurriedly shut her eyes. A moment later, firm hands touched her at the base of her ribs. Sun-block was smeared over her stomach, hot in the sun. The pushing fingers moved upwards, smoothing the skin over Shannon's ribs.

Shannon felt the tips of her fingers slip under the bottom of her bikini top. Laura's hands did not stop. The slick fingers slid up over the curve of her breasts. Her bikini top rode up. Laura's hands moved to cup and hold Shannon's breasts.

The fire in her groin was unbearable. Shannon opened her eyes. The young woman was kneeling above her, blocking the light which shone through her tangled black hair. Her strong hands still cupped Shannon's naked breasts. The pale pink nipples swelled as Shannon watched. Her own nipples hardened.

'I love brown nipples,' Laura said huskily. 'Your breasts are so beautiful.'

Shannon reached up and took the woman's right hand. She held it in her own, and plunged them down under the top of her bikini pants. The tender flesh of her stomach shivered at the sensation.

'You're a virgin with women, aren't you?'

Shannon stuttered. 'Yes. That is, not exactly, but . . .'

'I can always tell.' Laura's heavy brows flirted up. 'I'll tell you a secret. It's better!'

Her hand slid down the front of Shannon's bikini pants until the tips of her fingers touched Shannon's curling hair.

With a mischievous grin, the younger woman snatched her hand away.

'What?' Shannon blushed brilliant red.

'Oh, I love a woman who can blush. Two things.' Laura sat up on her heels. 'I want to swim in the sea. I want to be clean. And, it's not as romantic as you think on a beach. Sand gets everywhere!'

'What?' Shannon repeated, hot and bewildered.

'We can go up in the hillocks. There's grass there, it's nice. Meanwhile . . .' She sprang up and ran towards the sea, fleet and fit. Shannon stared, open-mouthed. Then she grinned.

She leaped to her feet and began to run.

Shannon caught up when the younger woman had splashed through the shallows, and slowed her stride in the deeper water. She dived cleanly and shallowly, and seized Laura's legs from behind. A flailing body tumbled over her shoulder and splashed into the water.

'I caught you!' Shannon whooped. She reached out and caught the string on the emerald bikini bottom and tugged. Laura squealed. The scrap of cloth floated away on curving waves. She dived after it.

Shannon romped after her, catching the bikini bottom and holding it over her head. Laura threw her arms around Shannon's stomach and rugby-tackled her over. Both women went back into the salt water with a terrific splash. Shannon heard applause from the beach.

She came up holding Laura in the circle of her arms. The woman's black hair sleeked to head like a seal. Her full, small breasts pushed softly against Shannon's own breasts. Shannon felt two lithe, strong legs lock

116

around her waist. Laura's groin bumped her, ground into her hip as the sea drove them together; and a wave knocked them under and apart. Shannon came up spluttering. Laura was already running up the beach. The woman was naked, bikini bottom in hand.

More sedately, Shannon followed.

She plucked her towel and bag from the sand and followed Laura into the hillocks.

Droplets of water slid down her shoulders, thighs, and calves. The wet cloth of her bikini bottom slid up between her swollen labia. She paused, tugged the garment down and off, and walked on, rubbing herself dry with the towel.

Away from the beach, it was cooler, but still hot. Nothing moved the air. The sound of the waves died. Bees hummed among the yellow flowers in the long grass. The ground under her feet was hot.

Shannon scrambled up one hillock. Another dip opened before her. Marram grass grew thickly along its sea-edge. Low, small-leafed bushes grew on one side. They made a line of shadow along the bottom of the dip. White flesh flashed in the shadow.

Cautiously, she slid down the side of the hillock.

Laura lay in the shade, on her back, one leg bent and drawn up at the knee. The hair between her legs was wiry and dark. Shannon, on hands and knees, reached forward to touch it. Her questing fingers met a springy softness. She pressed in. Laura's eyes were big in the shadows. They did not leave Shannon's face.

Shannon's fingers felt springy damp hair. The tips of her fingers slid into a hot, wet crevice. The woman made a sound, half gasp, half sigh. Her hands grasped Shannon's wrist and pressed her hand down and in.

Shannon lay carefully on the grass. Her hand thrust deep between the young woman's legs. With her other hand she reached out and grabbed Laura's breast.

117

'I want a woman,' Laura whispered. 'I want a woman who'll fuck me so I can't stand. I want *you*.'

Shannon closed her hand tight over the young woman's breast, squeezing it hard. Her fingers pushed up into Laura's ready sex. Hot flesh throbbed under her. Gently she slid her middle finger in. Hot juices flowed down her hand.

'Am I doing this right?' she whispered. 'I mean, I don't know if . . .'

'That's good. Oh, that's good. Do *that*.'

Shannon began to slide her finger into the younger woman's hot cleft. The breast under her hand swelled. She thrust her stiff finger in deeper, harder. Laura's hips began to lift and move. Her thighs clamped on Shannon's wrist, then loosened. Shannon added another finger, sliding them both into Laura's hot sex. She thrust rhythmically, clenching her other hand. Bulging breast flesh pushed up between her fingers. Without losing the rhythm of her thrusting fingers, Shannon lowered her head and took Laura's nipple in her mouth. So much larger than a man's nipple. It swelled as she sucked and teased it with her tongue.

Laura's hands flattened against the grass. Her back arched. The flesh of her sex convulsed around Shannon's hand. Her body bucked and thrashed as Shannon threw her other arm around her, and her head fell back, mouth open, and she gave a great gasping yell. 'Ahhhh!'

A gull shrieked overhead. Shannon glimpsed white wings against a blue, hazy sky.

The younger woman's sweat-soaked body collapsed against her. Slick skin burned hotly against Shannon as she fell back. They lay breast to breast, belly to belly, thigh pushing against thigh. Shannon's unsatisfied sex ached.

'Is that . . .?'

'That isn't it. Not by any means.' Again, Laura gave her dark-browed, wicked grin. 'Lie back, little virgin. I'm going to teach you how to fly.'

Grass flattened under her. Shannon stretched back. Her hips writhed. Shadow and sunlight flirted over her sweat-soaked body. The solid figure of the other woman blocked the light again, briefly; then she was dazzled as Laura ducked forward.

The black hair tumbled softly down over Shannon's shoulders as Laura leaned over her. The younger woman, propped up on locked elbows, lowered her head. Her pink tongue flicked out and caught Shannon's left nipple. A bolt of pleasure shot from Shannon's nipple direct to her sex. She lifted her hands to cup Laura's breasts, above her.

The younger woman lowered her body. Her mouth encircled Shannon's nipple. She sucked the breast into her mouth, flicking Shannon's nipple again with her tongue. Pinkness flushed Shannon's skin. She fiercely handled the flesh before her, the woman's shoulders, arms, back, breasts. She pulled Laura's head up and their lips met, tongues thrusting deep into each other's mouths.

With a gasp, Laura broke away. She smelled of salt and perfume, tasted of fire. Shannon flopped back. She felt Laura's hands slide down her ribs, across her stomach, down the insides of her thighs. They pushed her legs apart. Shannon wriggled, drawing her legs up slightly. A hot mouth nibbled at the sensitive flesh inside her thigh and she squealed.

Laura's mouth closed over her sex. The woman's lips sucked at her labia. A strong tongue thrust between them. She moaned, pushing her hips up. The tongue thrust deeper and swirled, sending little bolts of pleasure through Shannon's flesh. She gasped.

The tongue slid forward and up. Shiveringly

delicately, it touched her swelling clitoris. Shannon nearly screamed. Two fingers inserted themselves in her and thrust.

'Oh my God!' Shannon grabbed the woman's shoulders. Her fingers drove deep into the soft flesh. 'Oh God, I'm coming! Oh God, don't stop!'

Fat flesh – two fingers? three? – thumped up into her cleft. Shannon's filled sex convulsed. Waves of pleasure lifted her hips off the ground. She drove her body down on Laura's hand, fiercely milking the last spasm, and fell back drained.

'Oh . . .'

Somewhere outside her dizzy collapse, a woman's voice chuckled. Laura. Shannon opened her eyes to see Laura's face. Her too-wide mouth was grinning. Her lips were wet. She cupped Shannon's cheek with her hand.

'I want you more,' she said.

Shannon's sex twitched. 'Can you – can we – I mean, how long does this go on?'

Laura's eyes twinkled. 'As long as you like, lover. I'm no one-shot wonder. Hey.' She pointed at the spilled contents of Shannon's bag. 'Hey, why don't we take some holiday snaps? I'll give you my address.'

'I'll send you copies.' Shannon laid her cheek on the younger woman's belly. 'You can come up to London. We'll do . . . lunch.'

She nibbled her way down the soft skin of the woman's belly. Laura's springy hair tasted of salt and woman come. She thrust her tongue deep, seeking her swelling bud of flesh; teasing, touching, moving away. The heat between her own legs soared.

Shannon sucked Laura's clit. The woman reached down and thrust short-nailed fingers into her dripping heat. Though she would have sworn it was too soon, a swelling wave of pleasure thundered through

Shannon's heat-soaked body.

The shadows of gulls fell across them all the long July afternoon.

The train rattled and jounced under her. Shannon leaned back against the upholstery, bonelessly relaxed and replete. From time to time she opened her bag and touched Corey's camera. With deep satisfaction, she thought, Let her develop these, that'll teach her to think of me as a mouse!

Her mobile phone bleated.

'Yes?' She kept her voice quiet.

'It's me.' Pause. '*Me.*'

'Oh. *Tim.*' She was grateful now that there were few other travellers in the carriage. Her heart beat faster, her face flamed. 'I told you not to call me!'

His voice was light, sexy, utterly familiar. 'I know. Look, I can't talk right now. Can I see you? I have something important to ask you.'

'I – no. Yes.' She breathed in sharply. 'I suppose so.'

'I'll be at your place at eight.' The connection broke.

By half-past seven her terraced house was spotless. Shannon paced backwards and forwards in the living-room, the day forgotten. The whole downstairs had been knocked into one room by a previous owner. Sunlight shone in through the glass doors that led to the tiny garden. She glanced at the stairs.

I'll put clean sheets on the bed. No, I won't. It'll look as if I was expecting him to . . . oh, he won't even notice! Shall I do it? I might as well. But it might look wrong. I told him we were finished!

At eight-oh-one she was stripping the sheet and duvet cover off. She pulled new bedding covers out of the cupboard and pulled them on. Flick covered her cotton dress. She pulled it roughly over her head, opened the wardrobe, dragged out a skimpy black

121

party dress, and dragged it on.

He's late. Maybe he'll bring flowers. I told him not to come back unless he was prepared to – no, that was the time before. What does he *want*?

At half-past eight, Shannon was propped up on the sofa by the window. She had glass of red wine in one hand, and the remnants of last Sunday's newspapers in the other. When the doorbell rang, she didn't even jump.

She put the wine carefully down. Newspaper broadsheets spilled on to the carpet. She walked to the door and opened it. 'Tim.'

Same old Tim. White shirt, blue jeans; the out-of-office uniform. His old green car parked in the road directly outside. She looked up into his dark eyes. He looked slightly plumper in the face: well-fed, happier somehow.

'Hello.' She saw him register her dress and look puzzled. 'I didn't know you were going out. Never mind, I won't keep you long.'

Shannon stood back silently and let him into the house. She waited to see if he would notice she had taken down the framed prints he had given her.

As far as she could tell, he didn't even look at the walls.

She poured him a glass of red wine. 'Why have you come, Tim? What have you got to say to me that's important?'

He picked the newspapers off the floor and straightened and folded them. In anyone else it would have been a nervous mannerism. When he looked at her, however, he was beaming with an expansive good humour.

'I'm sorry, I probably made it sound more desperate than I meant. It would be an *enormous* favour. I couldn't think of anyone, and then I thought of you – I know you wanted us to stay friends, and this is the kind of thing friends do.'

Shannon stared at him. She turned away briefly, running her fingers along the spines on the bookshelves. When she felt more composed, she said, 'You're not coming back to me, then?'

He still had the smile that melted her.

'We can talk about that when I get back.' He grinned boyishly.

'Get back? Tim, I think you'd better just explain.'

'I'm taking Julia away with me on a month's holiday to Greece,' Tim said, 'to celebrate our reconciliation. The kids are at her Mum's. I wondered if you could drop in on the flat while we're gone, and feed the cats?'

Chapter Nine

THAT EVENING NADIA had decided to keep *Ephemera* open very late, to catch the summer tourist trade. When the bell jangled for what she decided was the very last time, however, she came out into the shop to find Shannon Garrett, words tumbling out of her mouth.

'Nadia, I'm going to kill him!'

'Mmm? Oh, no. This is Tim again, isn't it?' Nadia nodded to herself. She did her best to follow the flood of explanation. 'I thought you'd finished with him.'

'I have! I'm going to kill him,' Shannon finished. 'Then I'm going to cut off his balls and *post* them to Julia. She's welcome to him!'

Shannon stomped past her into the back of the shop. Nadia flipped the shop sign from OPEN to CLOSED, and locked the door. She replaced the green baize covers over the counters, hiding the pieces of 1950s costume jewellery from anyone who might think it worthwhile breaking in. She could hear the other woman's shout clearly from the shop's back room:

'Who does he think he *is*? 'We'll talk about it when I get back'. No, we won't! I'm sorry for Julia. I'd like to tell her just who she's been married to for the last eight years! But if she doesn't know by now, she must be even more stupid than I was!'

Nadia tugged the curtain across, shutting the front of the shop off from the rear room. She found the woman sitting by the open back door, a glass of Perrier in hand, black party dress rucked up to her knees in the streaming evening sun.

'In a way, I'm glad he did it.' Shannon raised her face. 'There's no danger of me forgetting what he's like now. Not after this! I tell you something, Nadia, I am *not* going to let him get away with this. Nobody's doing that to me!'

'Why don't you come home with me and have supper? I've got some bits and pieces in the fridge,' Nadia offered.

'I'd like that. Thanks. Oh,' the woman said, as she got to her feet, 'what about – you know? Have you done Corey's dare yet? What was yours?'

Nadia licked her suddenly-dry lips. 'Not yet,' she admitted. 'I've been thinking about it. A great deal.'

Thirty-six hours later, Nadia drew the red MG up on the Wiltshire country house's drive in a swirl of gravel.

I didn't expect to come back here again. It hasn't changed.

After she cut the engine, everything was silent.

She rolled the window down and sat listening. Birds began to sing in the high arch of the sky, above the shimmering full green tops of the chestnuts lining the drive. Hot noon sunlight dappled her face through the leaves.

This is too risky. This is *far* too risky. I know these people!

And, of course, that's Corey's point.

Corey's dare had been simple. *Try the last one again.*

Then she went on to name names.

How many times did I want to do this, when I was living here with Oscar? Hundreds. It would have been . . . unfair. Not discreet. How many times did I think, *If I weren't married*—

A warm breeze blew, bringing the scents of flowers up from the hall gardens. Nadia looked briefly up at the old sun-warmed brick of the main building. The doors were closed. Blinds were down on most of the windows.

Oscar never did like to be here in August. He always preferred London. Me? I could never get used to the green . . .

Suddenly decisive, she opened the MG's door and swung her legs out. Her heeled sandals dug into the gravel. The designer-label green silk shirt-dress slipped, exposing her slightly freckled shoulders. The sun burned her skin as she stood up. She put on her sunglasses, and tucked her car keys into her small, expensive clutch bag. One of the few outfits she had kept after the divorce.

Two brightly-coloured butterflies flickered across the air. She heard bees humming. The hands of the clock on the hall tower pointed to one-twenty.

Ignoring the main door, Nadia walked across to the wrought-iron driveway gates at the side of the hall. She pushed. The hot metal swung back from her hand. She walked in, the crunching of her heels the only noise in that hot silence. She kept moving, past the hall's curtained windows on her left, and the riotous colour of the garden on her right hand, approaching the corner of the building.

She rounded the corner. Immediately opposite her were the stables, single-storey workrooms and garages. A large green Rolls stood on the gravel. Half of it was covered in suds. A male voice was singing, not very tunefully. As she watched, a bucketful of water flew over the roof from the far side, and a man came around the back of the car, carrying a wash-cloth. Richard! she thought. You *are* still here.

He was about thirty; short, stocky and ruddy-faced. When he saw her, his face went momentarily blank. He grinned with equal amounts of surprise and pleasure. She registered the quick flick of his gaze up and down her body before he coughed, looked down, and automatically touched his finger to where his cap-brim would have been.

'Hello, Mrs Trevithic.' He hesitated. 'Sorry, ma'am. Miss, I mean.'

'It's not Trevithic now. It's Kay again. Hello, Richard.'

She straightened her shoulders. The thin silk of her dress strained a little across her breasts, as they swelled slightly with arousal. She looked at the chauffeur. His shoes were brightly polished, and the creases in his black uniform trousers knife-sharp. The only concession he had made to the heat was to take his uniform jacket off and roll up his shirtsleeves. He was wearing a dark blue tie. His sandy hair had been cut very short since the last time she had seen him, and it stuck up in tiny sweaty tufts.

'Mr Oscar isn't here, miss.'

'I know. He's in London.' Nadia walked forward. She rested her hand briefly against the wing of the Rolls. The hot metal burned her fingertips. She moved around and opened the back passenger door on his side of the car and sat down, her legs still outside.

Immediately she was covered in a thin film of sweat. The leather smell of the upholstery permeated the interior of the car. She looked up and out at the chauffeur. 'Aren't you hot, Richard?'

'Yes, ma'am. Miss.'

Nadia leaned back into the car, feeling the expensive

127

silk slide across her body. She stretched her legs out. 'Do you remember,' she said dreamily, 'all those times you drove me up to London, shopping? It seems so long ago now.'

'I didn't forget that yet, miss.' He scrubbed his big hand across his cropped hair. His eyes squinted against the noon sun. He reached up and tugged at the knot of his tie. His eyes dropped from her face, down to the vee-neck of her silk shirt-dress, down her body, to the long, bare silky length of her legs. 'Nobody's in the house, miss, you've had a wasted journey.'

'Not yet,' Nadia murmured. She made eye contact and held it. His face reddened. It might have been the sun. She rather thought not. She leaned against the back of the seat, stretching one leg, pointing her sandalled toe. Perspiration slicked her skin. If she left the car now she would find the baking noon cool by comparison.

'I used to watch you driving, Richard,' she said. 'Your hands on the wheel. You have strong hands; I like that.'

The blond man glanced at his hands and then put them behind him. He half-turned away and threw the wash-cloth. Nadia heard it splash into a bucket.

'I watched you too.' His voice was rough. He gave her no title. When she looked up, his face was hard.

'That was then,' she said. 'I won't be back here, Richard. This is just a last visit. I'd rather like to celebrate it. Please don't say anything if you feel you'd rather not.'

'My God.' His face above his white shirt collar burned bright red. 'My God, woman. You don't mean it.'

She looked at his strong-featured face. He had the same attractive innocence about his own male appeal.

'I don't say anything I don't mean,' Nadia said simply. 'I'd like to undress you, with my teeth.'

'I used to come home after I'd driven you around all

day, miss.' His voice thickened. 'You'd go into the big house with a dozen shopping bags. I'd go back to the garage and think about how you'd look with your knickers down around your ankles, or your face in my crotch. You got any idea how often I've fucked you?'

Nadia rubbed her palms over her sweat-slick cheeks. She pressed her hands to her sides, pulling the green silk taut across her breasts and stomach. She watched his member stiffen in his pants. It was as big as she had always imagined.

'Tell me what I did.' Her breathing quickened.

He pulled the knot of his tie loose with two quick tugs. He stood with his feet planted slightly apart, coiling the strip of material over one hand. He started to speak, mumbled, shook his head, and then met her gaze with dark hungry eyes.

'You'd be going to get out of the car,' he said roughly, 'and you'd pull your dress up. And you'd be wearing French knickers, silk ones, and I'd see them.'

Nadia drew one of her legs inside the Rolls. She left one outside, her toe touching the gravel. She shifted her buttocks on the leather seat. The green silk shirt-dress rode up her thighs. An edge of ivory silk showed. 'Then what would I do, Richard?'

'Then you'd part your legs,' the chauffeur said, 'so I could see up into your crotch.'

A pumping pulse of arousal went through her sex. Nadia put her clutch bag demurely down on the seat. Then she swivelled on the hot leather, spread her legs, and reached down and pulled her dress up to the very tops of her thighs. He gazed at the crotch of her ivory silk French knickers. Nadia felt herself growing damper. 'And then?'

'And then I'd push you back on the seat.' His strong hands gripped his tie, then threw it down on the gravel. He ducked his head and leaned into the car, pushing his body in. The strong scent of sweat came in with him. His bare forearms were covered in wiry golden hair. He put the palm of his hand on Nadia's left breast.

She eased back on to the seat, the leather upholstery hot under her skin. His hand slid down her dress, over her stomach, down to the pit of her belly. He took each side of her knickers between a thumb and forefinger. Nadia shut her eyes. She felt him pull the material down over her bottom, catching between her and the seat, and then her mound was bare.

'*Jesus Christ!*'

Nadia's eyes flew wide open. Richard's body blocked her view. He swore, backed out of the car, cracking his head on the door-frame, and swore again. He was stuffing his shirt back down the front of his unzipped trousers. Nadia sprawled with her legs apart, her damp sex feeling the summer air, her knickers around her knees.

The same new voice repeated, 'Jee-sus. . .'

'Lee?' Nadia lifted her head. 'Is that you, Lee?'

The newcomer was a young man of about twenty. He had a mass of dark yellow curly hair that fell below his broad shoulders, and the aquiline features of a fifteenth-century angel. His well-muscled chest was brown and bare. His strong legs and thighs were sharply defined under the well-worn soft denim of his jeans, so old they were more faded white than blue. To her joy, Nadia recognised the gardener's assistant Oscar had taken on a few months before their initial separation.

The fly of his soft denim jeans bulked hard and full as Lee gazed into the car. He flushed. 'Sorry, I – sorry, Miss Nadia.'

'Don't go.' Nadia caught Richard's gaze. 'Let's go into the stables. All of us.'

There was a moment's hesitation. Then Richard reached into the car and caught her hands. She came forward as he pulled, and he bent down and scooped his hands under her knees and arms, and set off towards the stable block with fast and powerful strides. She was dimly aware of Lee at the periphery of her vision.

The change from sunlight to stable left her dazzled for seconds.

She felt Richard lower her. Her body fell back against a sweaty bare chest. Hay stroked her legs. She was placed down on some surface that gave. Gazing up, she realised she was in an empty horse-box. Lee was behind her, supporting her upper body. Her legs sprawled wide apart on the hay-strewn floor.

Without preamble, Richard unzipped his fly. His erect cock bobbed out, thick and full. Nadia lifted her hands behind her and encountered the hot, shivering skin of another body. She dropped her hands into Lee's crotch. His prick swelled in his pants.

'Is this—' His voice cracked with anxiety. 'I mean – is this all right? Can we—'

'I always wanted you to fuck me.' Nadia's eyes accustomed to the dusty sunlit gloom. 'I used to watch you both out here. I couldn't do anything. Now I can say it. I want you both inside me.'

Richard knelt in front of her legs. She eased her hips up and slipped her knickers off. Lee's hands came down from where he knelt behind her head. His dirt-stained fingers fumbled with the buttons of her expensive silk dress. It fell open. He seized her breasts in their ivory satin bra cups. His fingers felt rough and calloused.

Richard's stubbled face pressed between her thighs. She felt his hot breath on her sex. Her flesh loosened and swelled. His tongue flickered into her inner lips.

Her back tightened and arched. Lee's mouth came down on hers. His strong tongue thrust between her teeth. Richard's tongue lapped up her sex, over her clitoris, up her belly, trailing saliva up to where Lee's strong wrists showed their corded tendons as he grasped her breasts.

Lee's long kiss ended. Nadia gasped in a breath. 'Every time I saw you in your uniform – every time I saw *you* in the garden – I longed to come up and grab your crotches and drag you in here!'

Lee's mouth dropped to her breasts. His sweating muscled torso leaned over her. He bit and nibbled down her body. Nadia reached up and unbuttoned the top of his jeans. She unzipped his fly. His waiting cock swung down and hung. She drew it down to her mouth and began to lick the shaft. It hardened between her hands. She kept his cock in her mouth, and moved her hands up his body, up his flat belly, to his nipples and the soft hair of his chest, as far as she could reach.

Without warning, Richard's cock pushed between the lips of her sex. She stiffened, then her relaxing flesh drew him into her hot wetness. His first thrust was a delicious fullness. She licked down the base of Lee's cock to his balls, burying her face in his scant soft hair. He smells of sweet grass, she thought, and licked him from balls to anus. His thighs parted, so that he straddled her body below the shoulders. Nadia looked up from between the tight cheeks of his ass, up the length of his muscled back, in time to see Richard put both hands either side of the boy's head, and thrust his tongue down the boy's throat. Richard's cock inside her leaped and swelled. She writhed her hips, moaning.

'Up!' Richard said wetly. He pulled at her with urgency. Not understanding, she was for a moment bewildered. Lee tumbled off. Richard's hands under her arms lifted her upright. Her sandalled feet sought a firm footing in the hay.

The blond man pushed her dress back off her shoulders. Her bra was unhooked from behind. Their hands were everywhere. Nadia felt herself stroked, handled, caressed, fondled, until she did not know who did what. Richard's hips pressed into hers, Richard's thick cock impaled her and held her up.

Something nudged at her anus. She gasped. Her body ran with salt sweat. A thick tongue pushed at the rim of her ass, pushing just inside and then retreating, softening her, making her ring of flesh open and then contract. She felt a handful of saliva smeared over her anus. Then with great and gentle care, Lee put the head of his cock at her entrance and pushed.

Richard's cock thrust up. She grabbed his shoulders to hold herself up, standing almost on tiptoe, even in the heeled sandals. The boy's cock pushed remorselessly in, penetrating her ass. She felt the shaft swell, filling her bottom. For one moment she stood in the hot sweating stable, bare from the waist up, with Richard's cock buried to the hilt in her pussy, and Lee's cock filling her ass.

'Fuck me,' she gasped.

'Now,' Richard grunted. Lee thrust. He thrust. Alternating, they began to pump her, lifting her up on to her toes. Nadia's eyes flew open wide. She lifted one leg and hooked it around Richard's thick muscular thigh for support.

'Oh, yes! Oh God. Do it to me,' she groaned. 'I always wanted this! In the car, on the back seat. In the garden, on my back on the grass. I wanted, I *want*. Do it!'

Richard's hands held her shoulders firmly. Lee gripped her hips. Richard's head was thrown back, his teeth bared, and she felt him swell hot and hard within her. The boy's lips brushed her freckled shoulders, and he began to bite at the skin, nipping and worrying a fold of flesh until it tingled, then licking, then seizing another mouthful. His silk-hard shaft pushed up, prising apart the ring of muscle at her anus. Richard's thrusting began to speed up. She was filled, impaled, bursting with their fullness.

'Oh yes!' She clenched her hands on the chauffeur's biceps. Now Lee's thrusts lifted her up on to her toes every time. Each of the men thrust and withdrew, thrust and withdrew, alternately; and her soft inner flesh grew more swollen, more hot, more full with every stroke. 'Oh yes, oh yes – *oh!*'

The two men thrust together. Two cocks simultaneously filled her. Hot come spurted up into her. Her sex exploded with a searing, intense, prolonged burst of pleasure that blackened her vision, weakened her knees, and left her collapsed back against Lee, head thrown back on his shoulders, arms spread wide, her hot sweat cooling on her bare breasts. Their shrinking cocks began to slip from her.

A voice from the door said, 'Am I interrupting at all?'

Nadia twitched as if stung. She lifted her head, otherwise helpless to move. A dark body leaned on the stable's half-door. With the sun behind him, his face was invisible. She recognised his voice instantly.

The customs officer from the banquet.

Nadia Kay shifted her weight forward. Her sweating skin unpeeled from the gardener's, behind her. She looked at the man who had been her chauffeur, standing with his uniform trousers around one foot.

'Thank you,' she said coolly, 'I believe that will be all.'

Once outside the stables, furiously buttoning her dress, she swung around to face the customs officer.

He was wearing off-duty clothes: soft denim jeans and a white T-shirt, which he filled well enough to catch her attention, and make her annoyed at herself for noticing. She demanded, 'How dare you! What do you mean by coming here! How did you find me?'

'It wasn't difficult to find out what you do. A lot of people at the function obviously knew you. This morning I found an elderly gentleman looking after your shop who said you'd gone into the country.' He shrugged massive shoulders. 'I guessed you might be visiting your old home. I wanted to see you again.'

Nadia finished buttoning her silk dress. She tugged the hem of the damp material firmly down over her thighs. 'Well, now you've seen me!'

Despite her immediate embarrassment, a sense of triumph reasserted herself. Her body hummed contentedly with pleasure: if she had been a cat she would have purred. Her pussy and her ass both throbbed with the afterglow of pleasure, sticky with sweet come.

I have taken my pleasure, she thought, no one can take that away from me.

The big man smiled cherubically down at her. 'I did you some good. The last time we met, the height of your ambition was to have two men in the same *bed*.'

He cocked an eyebrow.

'I've obviously helped you to become more ambitious.'

Nadia blushed. She caught herself stuttering. 'It wasn't like that! It *isn't* like that! This has nothing to do with you.'

'Really?'

'Yes. Really!'

He smiled beautifully. 'Must be a coincidence, then.'

'*What?*' Nadia stood and stared, outraged, as he turned and walked away.

'What makes *you* think *you're* responsible for what I dare do?' she shouted. Her voice echoed off the frontage of the hall. She felt her face colour. The big man did not turn around. He kept on walking. As he got into his blue Vauxhall Astra, she heard him start to whistle.

You did *me* some good—?

Of all the fucking nerve!

When she got back into the MG, she saw Corey's spare camera. Still on the back seat. Still in its case.

'Oh, *bugger!*' Nadia exclaimed.

A crow shot up from the front of the hall and flew away into the distance, squawking.

Chapter Ten

THEY RENDEZVOUSED AT the weekend at Corey's flat.

Comparing their photographic evidence turned out not to be an illuminating experience. Shannon Garrett held up a three-by-five inch print. She turned it around, held it upside-down, and studied the matt surface carefully. 'Is that his dick? I can't tell.'

'The light was bad,' Corey said grumpily. 'Here are yours. She hasn't got much in the tit area, has she?'

'That's *me*,' Shannon said frostily. 'She took one when she was on top. Look, they always look smaller when you're lying down! Don't they?'

'Naturally.' Nadia, Shannon noticed, spoke without smiling. She was sitting in the only chair in the bedroom/darkroom. The older woman prodded the curly strips of paper still glistening with the developing liquid, none of which were hers. 'Richard and Lee had wonderful bodies . . .'

'So you keep telling us,' Shannon muttered. 'There's no need to be so po-faced because you were interrupted.'

'That *man*—'

The doorbell interrupted them.

'You guys stay here.' Corey shifted herself up from the futon and padded to the living-room door. 'I'll deal with it.'

As the black-haired girl disappeared, Nadia looked down at Shannon where she lay on the bed. 'I defy anyone to win anything at all on the basis of photographs like these.'

Corey's screech cut her off. '*You want me to what?*'

Shannon exchanged glances with Nadia. She got up and moved towards the door between the bedroom and the main room, intending to close it.

A frosty voice in the living-room said, 'You heard me. My son has been selected to stand for Parliament. A seat in the Midlands, I believe. You'll remember his interest in politics.'

Shannon mouthed *Patricia* at Nadia, and the red-headed woman nodded, and padded over barefoot to join her. Shannon raised her brows. Nadia shook her head, and put her finger to her lips.

'Ben might as well be an MP.' Corey's tone from the other side of the door was scathing. 'He's stupid enough. What's this got to do with me?'

'He plans to stand as an MP. His constituency know he's divorced, and while they frown on it, they can live with it. The last thing I want are those dreadful media people finding out that he used to be married to some half-South American porn model.'

Corey's voice squeaked. 'I've never done porn in my life!'

'You surprise me.' The older woman's voice was icy. 'I have my son's respectability as my concern. Whatever kind of modelling it is you're doing, you are to stop it immediately.'

There was a pause. Shannon, biting her lip, put a hand on the door to the living-room. She felt her movement arrested and glanced down to see Nadia's hand on top of hers.

'You're out of your mind,' Corey mumbled.

Patricia Bright's voice echoed clearly. 'As far as I know, you shouldn't be carrying on a business out of this flat in any case. I understand your lease forbids commercial activity. Possibly your landlord is as yet unaware of what you do?'

Corey snarled, 'So how am I supposed to earn a living?'

'Really, that isn't my concern. I expect you'll find some other young man to take in with your lies, the same way that you took in my Ben. I think we understand each other, dear, don't you? I have to go now: I have to rehearse for my little talk at the Conway Hall. No, don't trouble yourself. I'll see myself out.'

The flat's front door closed with a click.

'We couldn't help hearing.' Shannon stepped into the living-room. 'The old bitch. Oh, Corey!'

She held out her arms as the younger woman burst into a short, furious rage of tears. Shannon hugged her. She was aware of Nadia pouring something into a glass and pushing it into Corey's hands. Corey stepped back, drank, and stopped crying, her face bright red.

'The bitch!' Corey drained the glass. 'OK, I can survive on my photography, but the modelling's only catalogue, it isn't even glamour or porn modelling, and in any case *it's the fucking principle!*'

Shannon manoeuvred the girl into sitting down on the old cane sofa. 'So I dare you to do a porn movie. That would show her.'

'She'd just have me evicted. She's got friends. I'm stuffed . . .' The girl wiped the back of her hand across her eyes and looked up. 'Oh well. Don't worry. I'll think of something.'

'Corey,' Shannon said.

'No, I mean it. Forget it. I'll phone Perry in the morning; tell him I can't make it. I don't want to think about it now.'

'I have an idea,' Nadia said.

Both the other women looked at her.

'Corey, sweets, your storeroom, do you still have the key?'

The black-haired girl glanced at the door at the corner of the far wall of the dormer bedroom. 'I guess so. Why?'

Nadia didn't answer. The girl got up and began to rummage through heaps of cosmetic jars, cheap Goth jewellery and small change on the top of her dresser. Eventually she held up a key.

'I wanted to have it done up as a darkroom,' she said. 'The landlord won't convert it into another bedroom; he might just as well have let me. There's nothing in there, Nadia.'

The red-haired woman uncurled from where she sat on her chair. She stood up lazily, as if the summer heat made her too languid to do anything at all, but Shannon saw there was excitement in her eyes.

'Give me the key.' Nadia took it. She crossed the room and unlocked the door.

Shannon padded after her, peering over her shoulder from the doorway.

The room beyond Corey's bedroom was an unconverted loft. Unlike the bedroom and living-room, the walls were not plastered, but were bare brick. The air was heavy and hot.

Corey reached around her and tugged a string. A bare bulb hanging from the rafters flared into harsh light.

Two tiny dormer windows had been let into the sloping roof. Cobwebs hung from the beams. The room was much longer than Corey's bedroom, and halfway down it was divided by massive wooden cross-beams, one diagonal, one horizontal at waist-height, and one just above floor-level. The rafters had been floored over at some time in the past. Old cardboard boxes were scattered across the floorboards: stacks of magazines tipped over, a non-functioning Hoover resting with its wheels up in the air.

'This will take your mind off your problems,' the red-headed woman announced. 'Corey, sweets, if you don't mind me making a suggestion about how some of your five thousand pounds is spent, I have an idea.'

When Shannon looked at Corey, the younger woman's face was bewildered.

'Well, OK. I guess. Oh, come on, Nadia!' Corey began to smile with anticipation. 'What is it? What's going to happen?'

Nadia prodded distastefully at the nearest cardboard box with her bare foot. 'First, you are going to clear this mess up. Shannon and I will then dust, brush, and scrub this room to within an inch of its life. It's a perfectly adequate room under all the dirt.'

Shannon said, 'Umm . . .'

'While we do that, Corey, you will go out and purchase a reasonable quality camcorder, and whatever you need for home development of the film.' Nadia shrugged her lithe shoulders, beaded with perspiration from the attic's airless heat. Her eyes gleamed. 'We don't yet have a winner of our little competition. It's proving impossible to get photographic evidence outside. Very well. I dare you – Shannon – all of us – to bring our dares back here! *Then* film them. Then we can really judge the winner!'

'What's *this?*' Shannon wiped the back of her hand across her forehead. She had reached the far end of the attic. Dust, wet with her own sweat, smeared her forehead.

Corey clomped across the bare boards. 'Oh, that. It's my old futon frame, the cheap one. I kept it as a spare. Let's put it up.'

A quarter of an hour later, Shannon looked at the bare slatted frame of the futon. She coughed, and sat down on its edge. 'This is far too much like hard work!'

Nadia rested her elbows on the cross-beam in the middle of the room. There was a wet circle on the hem of her summer dress, where she had been kneeling to scrub the floorboards. 'Corey, my dear, what a wonderful contraption. May I suggest a little more in the way of furnishings?'

The younger woman kicked the lowest cross-beam with her foot. 'I'd thought of a couple of ring bolts.'

'Ring bolts?' Shannon said. 'What for? Oh.' She coloured.

'What's wrong with having our very own dungeon?' Corey grinned. The expression faded, suddenly, and she sat down on the lowest beam. Nadia remained leaning on her elbows above her. The young woman said, 'We have to be a bit careful. I don't want any nutters knowing where I live. And I don't want my landlord finding out! The trouble is, Patricia's right. If he knew about the darkroom business, he'd go ballistic; as for *this*—!'

Nadia reached down and ruffled her short black hair. 'Don't worry, sweets, we're not stupid.'

'We'll handle the practicalities,' Shannon said. The futon frame was uncomfortable. She stood up. She looked around the cleared, swept, scrubbed dormer room. 'Who's going to be first?'

'Have we all thought of dares?' Nadia asked.

Corey reached into her jeans pocket and pulled out a handful of small change. She selected three coins, giving one each to Nadia and Shannon, and keeping the other for herself. 'Odd one out dares first,' she said.

'Heads,' Nadia announced.

'Tails,' Shannon said.

Corey lifted her hand off her twenty-pence piece. 'Heads. You then, Shannon.'

'I've got one for you, Corey,' Shannon said. Thinking ring-bolts, indeed! 'This *is* a dungeon. It only needs whips and chains! Let's use some of the money and go shopping . . . Then I dare you to put a card up in the phone box down the road, and have whoever comes along and phones in.'

Corey Black stood over Shannon, where the older woman knelt on the floor by the phone. She rested her elbows on Shannon's shoulders. Curly brown hair tickled her bare arms as she steadied the pair of binoculars.

'Got it,' she said crisply. 'OK, answer the phone.'

She felt Shannon's arm move as the woman lifted the receiver to her ear. 'Yes . . .?' Shannon purred.

The image in the binoculars sharpened. Corey focussed them on the telephone booth twenty yards down the road. It had transparent plastic walls, and she could clearly see the profile of the man inside it, handset in hand.

'Make him talk to you!' she whispered. 'What does he sound like?'

'Shut up!' Shannon put her hand over the mouthpiece. 'Ordinary. He sounds ordinary. *Yes, tell me more . . .*'

The man in the booth stood with his face to its wall, his back to the street. His posture was very upright. His hair was sandy red. He wore a white shirt, a tie, and smart grey trousers. There was a briefcase of some sort at his feet, possibly a jacket; she couldn't make that out.

'He says am I "Mistress Whip"?' Shannon whispered, between panic and hilarity. 'What shall I tell him?'

'Tell him you can arrange a meeting with her, dummy! Ask him what he likes.'

'This one doesn't look too strange, then?' Nadia enquired from the back of the room.

'Normal as hell. Not that that means anything. Wait a sec . . .' Corey focussed on his face. He was fair-skinned, freckled, and slightly baby-faced, so that it was impossible to tell if he were in his early or his late twenties. Fairly tall. Stocky. His reddish-orange hair had a slight curl and was cut short. He shifted his feet, altering his position, and Corey got a clearer look at his features. Well-shaved cheeks, appearing almost scrubbed, with a slight pink tinge. Wide eyes. Very definite jaw and nose, but then, something about his mouth as he talked . . .

She saw the distant figure lift his hand up to the wall of the phone booth. He took down a card – ours! she thought. And now there was no mistake, his face was very pink.

She lowered the binoculars and remembered to whisper. 'What's he like?'

'He says his name's Adrian and he likes "the usual".' Shannon had her hand over the mouthpiece again. 'He says his "safe word" is *blue*. What shall I *tell* him?'

Corey shook her head. 'Look at him. Too tame.'

Nadia came forward out of the shadows. 'Shannon, it's your dare, you decide.'

The telephone handset that Shannon held began to yelp with indistinguishable speech. She leaned over Corey's shoulder, one hand steadying herself. 'I think so, yes.'

'What?' Corey protested. 'He's uptight as hell, look at him!'

'Then he may just be a challenge. The dare is, after all, to *make* a man come.' Shannon smiled. 'I'm going to tell him to go to the junction, turn left, turn left again, go into the yard where the garages are, and stand with his face to the wall until someone comes for him.'

Corey raised the binoculars again. 'Challenge. Yeah. Right . . .'

Adrian Ryan stood facing a brick wall. The noon sun cast his shadow at his feet. Sweat ran down the back of his neck. He felt in his trouser pocket for a handkerchief. Suppose someone comes? he thought, wiping his face. People must get their cars out all the time. What am I going to say if someone asks me what I'm doing?

It had been a momentary impulse. Needing to make a phone call on the way back to the Inland Revenue office, he had pulled his car up beside the phone box purely because it was unoccupied. The picture on the white card tucked behind the call board had attracted his attention.

'Stand right where you are,' a female voice said behind him.

His body jerked with surprise. He straightened his shoulders and resolutely stayed facing the wall.

Something hot and smelly dropped over his head. It felt like sacking. A hessian bag? He couldn't see out of it. He lifted his hands to his face.

Something sharp whipped across his knuckles. He yelped.

'I didn't say you could touch that.' The voice was grim. 'Now turn around. And move when I tell you to!'

A hard object poked him in the small of the back. He stumbled forward a surprised step.

'Move!'

Blindfolded and uncertain of his footing, he began to walk. Now it was too late for such doubts, he was suddenly reluctant to proceed. Previously his adventures had been confined to areas on the continent. Or at any rate, outside London. Away from home.

The hard object poked him in the back again. 'Keep moving!'

Corey pulled the heavy curtains over the dormer windows. She switched on the electric light. The bare bulb swung. The bare frame of the spare futon stood alone in the middle of the floor. The only other furniture now was the heavy cross-beams across the centre of the room, with their thick metal ring-bolts.

The last thing she did was check the video camera was recording.

'She's got him!' Nadia whispered from the bedroom door. 'Is the mobile phone on? We'll be in the car. If there's any trouble, shout.'

Corey grinned at the older woman. 'You still don't think I'll go through with this? It's not me who's in trouble. It's him! Whoever he is.'

The outside door opened. Nadia held her finger to her lips. She silently pulled open the bedroom door and allowed Shannon to come in. A man preceded her. He had a casual jacket on now. Folds of thick sacking had been thrown over his head.

'Stop!' Shannon snapped. The man halted instantly. Shannon broke into a huge grin. She reached past him and handed Corey the short-thonged whip. Corey waved both of the other women away. Both of them backed out of the room in exaggerated silence, tiptoeing. Corey marched over and slammed the door.

His whole body startled.

Corey paced back across the room until she stood in front of the blind-folded man. She bent down and picked a pair of padded manacles off the bed. Then she gripped the man tightly by his left wrist. His muffled head swung wildly, as if attempting to see.

He didn't try to take the bag off. He didn't move his arm.

His wrist was thick and corded with muscle. Corey snapped one manacle shut around it. She reached over and grabbed his other wrist.

'H-hello?' he whispered.

The second manacle snapped shut and locked. Eighteen inches of chain swung between his two wrists.

'Hello, is anyone there?'

She took a firm grip on the metal chain and yanked. He stumbled forward. She prodded him with the whip handle, steering him through the door into the far room.

Corey reached up and snatched the sacking off his head.

The man blinked, staring around wildly. Close up, he might have been five or six years older than her. His red hair was ruffled up by the sacking. His face shone pink and hot. He blinked, and then his eyes fixed on her.

Corey put one hand on her hip. She let the thongs of her whip trail down her thigh. She wore extremely tight leather jeans. She saw his eyes move down to her high-laced combat boots, and then back up to the heavy-buckled belt at her waist. Above it, her breasts were tightly lashed into a leather bustier. It laced up, and it was at least a size too small. Her white flesh squeezed out from between the lacing, and her breasts were pushed up high out of its cups.

Her black hair was slicked straight back. She wore mirrorshades.

'Oh dear.' The man's tenor voice was unsteady. 'I'm

147

very sorry. I think there's been some kind of a mistake.'

Corey said nothing. She looked him in the eyes. He stood with his manacled hands held slightly away from his body, as if they had nothing to do with him. The colour had left his cheeks.

'Mistake,' he repeated. 'This sort of place . . . I didn't understand, or I wouldn't have come here. It's a mistake.'

'Oh, I don't think so.'

She saw how he almost flinched at the sound of her voice. 'What do you mean? Please, take these things off me.'

Corey kept her gaze on him. She walked a few paces to the left, a few paces to the right, the thongs of the whip stroking her leather-clad thigh. 'So it's a mistake, is it? I'll tell you what. You say to me, "I swear I don't want to be in chains," and I'll take them off you.'

She waited.

His gaze dropped. After a moment, a tide of red rose up out of the neck of his shirt. It flamed his cheeks, and he coloured right up to his hairline.

'No!' he protested finally. 'I *don't* want to be! This sort of thing doesn't do anything for me!'

'And you just phoned out of curiosity. Just to see what it's like. And now you're here,' Corey purred, 'you don't like it. The little boy wants to go home.'

He had very pale blue eyes, she saw, as he lifted his head again. They flashed now. 'Let me go!'

'Don't you think it's a little bit . . . late . . . for that?'

He backed away slowly, staring at her as if hypnotised. The bare brick wall hit him smack between the shoulder-blades. She noticed he didn't try for the door. Safe word, she reminded herself. *Blue.* Hey. He's really into this. This is going to be easy.

This is going to be fun.

She swung the whip against her thigh. The dozen thongs lashed the leather. He winced. She felt a spreading warmth in the pit of her sex. Her eyes began to gleam.

His voice rose. 'You can't keep me here against my will!'

Corey took three paces forward across the bare floorboards. She reached out and caught the chain of the manacles, and jerked it suddenly towards her. She didn't have to pull hard. The stocky man came forward with her movement. He tripped, then, and fell to the floor in front of her. Corey released the chain.

'Don't—' He rolled on to his back. His manacled hands went over his head.

She stood over him and kicked his hands away. 'I didn't give you permission to speak. I didn't give you permission to move. I certainly didn't give you permission to come here with your pathetic little excuses and expect me to believe you. *Get up!*'

He scrambled back on to his feet with his tie askew. The top button of his shirt burst open. Dust marked the knees of his grey slacks. Corey lifted her hand. He quite definitely flinched.

Safe behind the mirrorshades, Corey smiled like a shark. She finished her movement. She tugged his tie straight, and pulled up the shoulder of his check jacket where it was slipping down. She patted his cheek, once, just hard enough to sting.

'Why so worried, little man? I haven't done anything to you – yet.'

'I have to get back to work.'

'I don't think so.'

'You *can't* keep me here!'

'Oh, but I can. Forever, if I like. You don't even know where you are.'

Corey moved a pace closer. The hot, enclosed

dormer room brought a sheen of sweat to her flesh. She stood close to him, her breasts almost touching his chest. His eyes flicked downward. Then he shut them and turned his head away, blushing furiously. Something nudged against Corey's leather-clad stomach.

She let him see her look down and stare at the hard-on in his pants. When she raised her gaze once more, his face was burning. He squeezed his eyes shut.

'You've been lying to me . . .' She let her voice caress him. Then she snapped, 'Down!'

'What?' He opened his eyes. 'I don't know what you mean.'

'Yes you do. You're going to be punished for coming here. You're going to be punished for lying about coming here. And you're going to be punished a *lot* for getting hard without permission. It's all adding up, *boy*.' She let the last word crack. 'What have you got to say for yourself?'

He hung his head sulkily. 'Nothing, I suppose.'

'I don't think you understand where you are,' Corey said. She let the silence stretch. Then, softly, she said, 'You're mine, now.'

He raised his head. His eyes met hers. He moved his hands apart to gesture, and the manacle chain snapped taut, restraining his wrists. He opened his mouth as if to speak. Corey stared him in the eye, knowing he saw only faceless mirrorshades. His colour had subsided now. He paled.

'Please . . .'

Slowly, awkwardly, he sank to his knees on the bare boards in front of her. He bowed his head. His knees were apart, his chained wrists hanging between them. She had to strain to hear his voice. It was barely a whisper.

'Please.' He held up his chained wrists. 'Please! Let me go.'

She said nothing. She waited. At last he forced himself to look up at her. He was sweating again, and his eyes were wild. The lump in the front of his trousers was bigger than before.

Huskily, he said, 'What are you going to do to me?'

'I'm going to give you a lesson. I'm going to teach you to speak the truth.' Corey reached down to grab his chain. Her straining breasts in the leather bustier brushed across his face. She heard him gasp. She twisted her hand in the chain and tugged it up. He staggered to his feet.

She gave him a hard shove. He staggered towards the centre of the room. Corey followed, leisurely. He backed away from her. One of the cross-beams arrested his progress. His heels skidded on the boards, as if he would have backed away through solid wood if he could.

'Now drop your pants,' Corey ordered.

'What?'

'You heard me.'

He drew himself up. Now she was close, it was very apparent he was bigger and heavier than her. She let herself smile.

'You know my name,' she said softly. 'What is it?'

The man, Adrian, locked gazes with her. A stranger, in these few minutes grown very well known: the ruffled, sweaty hair falling into his eyes, the weak mouth, the body that almost imperceptibly trembled. After a minute his shoulders slumped. ' "Mistress",' he said.

Her sex throbbed. I've learned, she thought. And one of the things I've learned is, turnabout is fair play.

'I think I'll punish you for not using my name before,' Corey said. 'And for not obeying all my orders, instantly. You *will* obey me. Do you really want to find out what I'll do if you disobey me again?'

This time his voice was clearer, if no louder. 'No, mistress.'

'Then drop your trousers when I tell you!' She smiled. 'I'm not going to do it for you. You're going to do it all on your own.'

She stroked the thongs of the whip up between his thighs. His face paled, and he gasped. The crotch of his trousers strained. In acute discomfort, he said, 'But, mistress, you see what a state I'm in.'

'I didn't tell you to talk!'

She flicked her wrist. The dozen short thongs of the whip lashed, catching him across the front of both his thighs. His cock jumped in his pants.

'I'm sorry!' he gasped. He lifted his chained hands to his trouser belt. He stopped. 'You're not – the mistress isn't even going to look away?'

'Drop your pants.'

He unbuckled his belt. Reluctantly, he unzipped his fly. He shot an imploring glance at her. Corey remained impassive. Slowly, he pushed his trousers down from his waist. They slid down to his ankles. His body was white, his legs long, hard and hairy. Now all he wore below the waist were white boxer shorts, with a huge erection poking out of the front of the material.

'Did I give you permission to do that?' She pointed at his cock.

'No, mistress. I can't help it!'

'Why not?' She grinned at his silence. 'I know why. You know what I'm going to do to you. And you want me to do it. You're hard because you want it. Isn't that right?'

'No,' he protested furiously. His colour was high. He stood with his trousers around his ankles, wrists chained together. 'I don't want anything done to me!'

Corey reversed the whip and slid the hard handle

up the inside of his hairy thigh. She slipped it under the leg of his shorts, and pushed it between his legs, pushing aside his balls. She felt with the hard end of it for his anus. Holding the handle between his legs she grinned, and very slightly lifted.

'No!' He was up on the balls of his feet. His back rubbed against the wooden cross-beam.

She teased the puckered hole with the end of the whip handle. His legs clamped together and his eyes jammed shut. In a strangled voice he whispered, 'Mistress, no!'

'Yes.' She drew the whip handle out. Very lightly, she lashed him across the front of his shorts, and his huge erection. He gasped and bit his lip.

She hooked the handle of the whip over the front of his boxer shorts and pulled them down. The material hung up on his cock. She yanked it free. His erect cock was not large, no more than five inches long, but it was fat and purple and thick. The head oozed a drop of clear liquid.

'Turn around,' she said softly.

He shuffled round, his feet tangled in his clothing, until he was facing away from her. A hot pink colour crept up the back of his neck. He stood there in shirt, tie and jacket, his hands chained, naked from the waist down.

Corey roughly pushed him forwards over the horizontal bar. It was high enough to catch him across the stomach. He bent forward, his buttocks straining. Swiftly Corey ducked under the bar. She rapidly unlocked one manacle, yanked hard, threaded the chain doubled under the lower beam, and locked it around his wrists again. It brought him much further up over the bar. He grunted as he rose on tiptoe.

Swiftly, she cuffed his ankles to the lower beam, threading the chain through ring-bolts. He could move his feet perhaps eight inches apart, no more.

Adrian jerked his hands. The chain had no slack, it was absolutely taut. Now that his hands were chained under the second bar, he was completely unable to straighten up. She saw him realise this. The bar she had bent him over was high enough to be uncomfortable.

'Listen—' He twisted his head round, saw her face, and added, 'um, mistress. I've been punished. You don't have to punish me any more. I suppose I've been humiliated. Now you can just let me go, all right?' His voice lifted on a slightly aggressive note.

Corey smiled. 'You're not very bright, are you?'

She walked behind him, where he would find it difficult to see her, and studied his jutting arse. His hard cock was being crushed between his belly and the wide wooden bar. All the muscles of his legs were under tension as he strained upwards with his toes to keep his body from painfully crushing his cock.

'You're still lying to your mistress,' she said.

'I'm not!'

Corey turned around. She lay down on the bare frame of the futon, on her side, where she could study his upside-down red face. She could see it between his legs. Slowly she undid the buckle of her belt.

She said, 'I'm not going to do anything to you now. Until you beg me to.'

His hot, flustered expression did not benefit from being upside-down. Chains scraped wood as he wrenched his wrists from side to side. One toe slipped. He groaned and scrabbled for a foot-hold, trying to take his body-weight off his cock and balls.

Corey slid her hand down the front of her leather jeans.

'Nothing,' she said, 'until you beg me to do it. And you have to say every word.'

'*Let me go!*'

'No, I don't think so.' Her fingers slid down under the taut leather. The tip of her middle finger found her clitoris. She began slowly to rotate her hand. She could not keep her hips still. She did not try.

'Stop it,' he yelled. 'Oh God, stop it, you're making me hard!'

Corey arched her back. Spasms of pleasure flooded her sex. She withdrew her hand.

'I don't hear you asking,' she said lightly. She re-buckled her belt and began stroking the thongs of the whip between her thighs. Suddenly she rolled over and stood up.

'That's me done.' She jingled the key. 'Sure you don't have anything to say? OK. I'll unlock those cuffs, then.'

'What? No! I mean – that is – oh, hell!'

He slumped forward over the bar.

'Yes?' she enquired.

He said something inaudible.

Corey squatted down beside him. 'I don't think I heard that.'

'I said, I want you to do it.' Colour flamed under his skin. He was sweating. 'Mistress, please. Don't make me say it. Don't humiliate me like this!'

'Tell me that you want it.'

His voice dropped to a rough whisper. 'I – yes. All right, damn you! I want it!'

'Now tell me what you want me to do to you. In detail. Out loud. Otherwise – nothing.'

He hung over the wooden beam, his wrists shackled to the floor. Two buttons had come off his shirt now, and that garment and his jacket were soaked with sweat. His tie had come undone. His bare white bottom jutted up over the bar, and his trousers and pants tangled around his ankles. His taut legs shook with the strain of supporting himself on tiptoe. He hung his flushed, sweating head down.

He forced the words out. 'I want you to whip me.'

'How?'

'Hard,' he whispered.

'Where?'

'On my arse, and on my cock and balls.'

'And why?'

He squeezed his eyes tight shut. 'Because I get hard when you humiliate me, mistress. Damn you, do it to me, *I like it!*'

'Six of the best!' Corey snapped the whip. The short thongs lashed his taut, quivering buttocks. A bright pink stripe burned against his white skin. She drew her hand back. The second blow lashed his other buttock. His body jerked, leaping up from the bar.

'Filth!' she snarled. 'Scum!'

'Yes!' he yelled. 'I am! Please, no more, no more!'

'Too late now.' She drew her arm back to her shoulder and lashed down. The flesh on both his buttocks burned pink. His cock swelled against the wooden bar, and he forced himself up on the toes of his brown shoes. Corey flicked the thongs lightly against his balls.

'I told you, you're mine. Anything I want to do to you, I'll do. And you're going to kiss the whip afterwards and thank me – aren't you?'

'Yes!' His body bucked to the lash. Now he squirmed away from the leather. His buttocks and thighs glowed pink.

As Corey lifted her hand for the last time and lashed him across both buttocks, his legs straightened, his chains drew taut, his body momentarily came free of the bar, and a stream of come sprayed up in an arc from his straining cock. His hips banged the wood as he pumped, hard, in the final spasms.

'Oh God . . .' He sank down until only the chains

and the wooden bar kept him from falling to the floor. White come spattered his shirt and jacket, and dripped from his face.

Corey thrust her fist and the whip under his nose.

When he could speak, he muttered, 'Thank you, mistress.' His lips touched the whip handle.

Corey knelt down and took the manacles off his wrists. He collapsed on to the floorboards.

While he was still there, on his back, chest rapidly rising and falling, she bent down and took the white card out of his inside jacket pocket.

'What?' he raised his head.

Corey shredded the card and tossed it into a corner of the room. She smiled. He still hadn't seen her eyes, or her face, properly. All he could see were reflections in her mirrorshades of his own dishevelled body.

'Won't the mistress see me again?' He rose up on to his knees with difficulty. She realised he was not so much kneeling to her as momentarily unable to get up. His voice changed. 'You're . . . Look, let me come and see you again. I don't care what you want, you can have it. Just – let me come back.'

She looked into his pale blue, desperate eyes. She began to smile. She threw him the hessian sacking. 'Put that on, little boy.'

She reached out and turned the mobile phone off before she said, 'You might be back. You can always dream.'

Chapter Eleven

THE SCREEN FLICKERED to silver-grey as Corey Black's videotape ran out.

Shannon became aware that she was squirming in her seat. She stood up abruptly, and crossed her living-room to pop out the tape.

I never thought I'd be turned on by that sort of thing. But then, when we were listening to it over the mobile phone . . .

The sound quality on the video was distorted: you couldn't tell it was Corey's voice. Sitting in the Rover, on the sun-hot leather upholstery, it had been very clear that it was the younger woman's voice. Both she and Nadia had sat silently listening, first with curiosity, then distaste, then amusement; and then with what Shannon recognised in herself as growing arousal.

Nadia had not spoken. She had pressed the button and put the window as far down as it would go. The midday streets were hot. There was no cool breeze.

As a dare, it's going to take some beating. And I bet it cheered Corey up after that visit from Patricia!

Shannon Garrett stood in her terraced house living-room. She tapped the edge of the cassette tape case gently against her lip. An idea flickered across her mind – almost too quick to catch.

She began to smile. A slow smile, but it grew until her lips pulled back wolfishly from her teeth. She nodded her head. *Yes. Oh yes. If we can bring it off. . .*

It took her two goes to key Nadia Kay's number on the dial-recall.

'Nadia? It's Shannon. Yes. Look, I've had an idea, and I know how to make it work, it just came to me in a flash, the whole thing, I just – what? OK. Slowly. I've had an idea. Yes, it's a dare. No, for Corey. I know, but I think she'll like this one. I want to talk it through with you first, though.

'Why will she like it? Because I *think* I've just solved her problems with her ex in-laws.'

'It'd never work!' Corey gaped. 'And how are you going to—'

'Leave the practicalities to me.' Shannon grinned.

'I've already done a dare!'

Nadia Kay said, 'Then it gives you an extra chance to win. What do you say? Don't tell me Shannon's come up with a dare too outré even for you?'

Corey narrowed her blue eyes. 'I'll take that as a compliment. Look – if you prove to me this can be done, I'll do it! But I don't see *how*.'

Ben Bright checked his stride when he saw the white paper caught under the Saab's windscreen wiper.

'Not another damn ticket!' He opened the door and slung his case on to the back seat. Then he reached over the hood and tore the paper out from under the wiper. He bent down slightly to glance at the wheels.

No clamp.

Well, then, things could be worse. And the paper was just that, just a sheet of paper without a plastic cover – fly-sheet advertising, no doubt. Now he came to look, most of the cars parked nearby appeared to have a copy under their wipers.

'Bloody nerve!'

His brain registered the words written on the paper just as he crumpled it up. He stopped. Carefully he unfolded the ball of crumpled paper. A photocopy, yes.

Half a dozen words were followed by a mobile phone number.

Ben slowly sat down in the driver's seat. After a minute he pulled his legs into the car and shut the door. Metal and glass enclosed him in a soundless world. He stared out through the windscreen at the sunlit London road. The pedestrians walking past him might have been on Mars.

I swore I wouldn't do it again. Someone might find out. I can't risk it!

His cream-coloured Armani suit was light enough for the summer day, crisp and creaseless. The knot of his silk tie felt momentarily constricting. He put both hands on the wheel, looking at his Rolex watch.

I could spare two hours. If they could take me now. The amount I can pay, they can damn well take me!

He reached out for the mobile phone.

It took him half an hour of cutting up London traffic, the cooler on full blast, before he found the back street to which he was being directed. The usual run-down area. Almost leafy. A line of houses subdivided into flats and maisonettes; nearly-new cars with off-road parking on concrete frontages.

He parked the car two streets away. The briefcase got locked in the boot. Nothing much of interest in it. He removed from the boot a full sports-bag.

All right. I doubt that I completely discarded the idea that I would do this again. Otherwise why would I keep the bag here?

Bright sunlight dazzled off the pavements. He put on his Raybans. He walked through a darker world, looking for the flat number. There was no name under the bell. He buzzed and gave his first name. The lock clicked open.

The stairs inside were moderately clean. A skylight illuminated the stairwell. His shoes made no noise on the threadbare carpet as he climbed to the top floor. A familiar tightness in his breathing made him stop, and stare upwards.

I can go back. I'm not going to do this again, am I? Oh God, I swore I wouldn't! If Mummy ever finds out. . .

The sports-bag bumped his leg. Prompted, he began to climb again, until he stood on a small landing on the third floor.

Something lay on the mat outside the door. A silk scarf, long and black. There was a piece of paper lying on top. He picked it up, recognising the same handwriting that had printed the handbill. It was succinct.

Put on the blindfold. Knock.

Excitement curdled in his stomach. The same sensation that he had had as a child, when the roller-coaster at the fair winched its way up to the top of the rails and he sat gripping the bar, knowing that now it was too late, there was no way out, he was helpless in the face of the inevitable plunge over the edge.

He put down his bag with shaking hands. He bent and picked up the silk scarf, and wound it around his eyes. He knotted it. Then he reached out and fumbled for the memorised position of the bell. It rang loudly enough to make him jump.

He could not tell the moment when the door opened, if it did. He only knew it must have opened when a hand took his arm and pulled him forward. No word was spoken. He felt himself treading on carpet, then on bare boards; walking quite a way, but he was disorientated now. The hand left his arm.

'Just a moment,' he said. 'Let's discuss your rates and my preferences, before we go any further.'

A husky voice behind him said, 'The ad told you what gets done here. Didn't it?'

Ben Bright swallowed, hard. At last he managed to say, 'Yes. Yes, it did.'

The voice – no, another, different voice – said, 'Then you know all that you need to know. Sit down. Relax. Make yourself comfortable. She'll be ready for you in about five minutes.'

A door closed. He pulled the restraining silk scarf off over his head, in time to see that. Not in time to see who had shut it, they were gone. He nervously finger-combed his hair straight.

The room was hot. Bare brick walls at both ends, rafters and plaster above, and bare planks underneath. Obviously a dormer room, but swept and clean. Curtains shrouded the windows. A high-wattage bulb burned. Horizontal wooden cross-beams divided the room halfway down.

Ben brushed the cream cuffs of his Armani suit. There was a futon base on the floor, the wooden slats bare. A high-backed wooden chair stood beside it. Next to that, on a small table, a large jug of clear liquid and ice stood with a glass. He crossed the room, poured some out, and tasted it. Water. There was a small flask, which proved to contain coffee; and a cup. Apart from that, nothing.

His Rolex ticked the passing time away.

As always, he began to take fright. What if they're a crooked set-up? What if they've just – gone away? He did not quite dare try the door. He sat on the wooden chair and drank the water, and then, as time went by, the cooling coffee. No sounds came from the other room.

And what about the sports-bag, containing his change of clothes? He should have made it clear he wanted to change into his favoured old suit first.

How can they treat a paying customer like this? It's ridiculous! Anger gave him courage to approach the door. He heard noises from the far side of it.

'Put the blindfold on, lovey,' a woman's voice called. It was oddly reassuring how motherly she sounded. Ben pulled the silk scarf out of his pocket and re-fastened it. He heard the door open.

A hand took his arm again. It did not lead him out of the room he was in. Instead, he was sure, it led him further down into the centre of that room. A tug on his sleeve arrested his progress. Something hard banged his shin. He swore, coarsely. Something hard and metallic clamped around his right ankle. There was a harsh, metallic *clang!*

'Oh, now, look!' He reached up with both hands and pulled the silk scarf down. 'That's *quite* enough. This is ridiculous. You haven't even asked me what I want—' His voice died away as it caught up with his brain.

Two women faced him. Both wore identical jeans and summer T-shirts, of blue denim and white cotton. The one on the left was taller and slimmer. Other than that, he could not tell them apart. Both had the hairy heads and fanged muzzles of wolves.

Ben stared at the women wearing the joke-shop werewolf masks.

He went to take a pace forward and wrenched his leg. He looked down.

'Good – God!' There was a chain going through a ring bolt on the lowest wooden beam. It pulled taut between the ring bolt and his ankle. Around his ankle, over his dark blue silk sock, was a fleece-padded metal cuff an inch or so thick. He jerked his leg hard. Even with the padding, the metal dug painfully into his skin. 'Take that off me, you bitches!'

He swung round, breathing heavily. The two women had not moved.

Then he saw that one of them was holding a palm-sized camcorder.

'Put that down,' he said authoritatively. 'Right, I want that turned off *now*, do you understand? I thought you'd learnt better in this kind of business! What about client anonymity?' he bristled.

The taller woman spoke softly. The latex wolf mask blurred her voice. He could just make out her words. 'We find our clients pay well – for anonymity.'

'Oh, that's it, is it? You think you can blackmail me.' His confident tone was a triumph of effort. He shrugged, and leaned back nonchalantly against the waist-high wooden beam. 'Go ahead. Nothing's going to happen. You can't *make* me cooperate.'

At that, the shorter of the wolf women went over to the table. She upended the water jug. Only one drip fell out on to the dusty floorboards. Her louder and harsher voice said, 'You already have cooperated, I'd say. Wouldn't you?'

'I would, yes.'

'What?' Even without seeing either of their faces, he could hear from their tone that they were grinning. Smirking. It began to infuriate him that he couldn't see them. He took a firm pace forward. The chain jerked taut. He almost fell. 'Bloody damn bitches!'

One folded her arms. The other adjusted (with some difficulty, because of the mask) the focussing of the camcorder.

Ben Bright felt a heaviness in his bladder.

Sweat broke out over his forehead. No, no, not like

this! His mind protested; and some distant, traitorous part of his brain whispered slyly. But this is what you came for. You always swear you'll never do it again, and you always, always do. Why not – enjoy it?

'No!' He didn't know who he shouted at, himself or the masked women. He shifted uncomfortably from foot to foot. 'I, um, I want you to take this thing off my leg. We can talk about money, whatever you want, just – I want to leave the room.'

'That's sad,' the soft voice whispered through a wolf-mask.

'Tough,' the abrasive one said.

The pressure from his bladder became an undeniable strain. Something in the water, he thought wildly. One part of his mind admired the set-up of the operation. *Golden showers*, the hand-bill had read. *Toilet training and discipline*.

'Just get the damn camera out of here!' he hissed. 'Look, you've obviously got a very professional operation here, which I'll pay well for, just turn that thing off!'

The taller and thinner of the masked women moved down the room. He noticed she stayed well out of arm's reach.

'Look,' he said, 'let me go. You haven't let me change. For God's sake, this is an Armani suit! This isn't fair. You know I'd pay you well for the real thing, done properly. Look, I know you've put something in the water. Let me get changed quickly.'

He became aware that he was shifting from foot to foot. He forced himself to stand still. The pressure in his bladder was now a pain. The whole bottom half of his body tensed.

'Put your hands behind your back,' her voice said behind him. He hesitated. She said, 'Do you want to be freed or not? Do it!'

'I don't see how, what . . .' Reluctantly, he placed his hands in the small of his back. 'What are you doing? What – no!'

Two smart metal clicks sounded. He furiously yanked his wrists apart. Unpadded metal cut into his skin. He swore. He tried to lift his arms over his head, and failed; tried to push them down where he could step over them, and became helplessly entangled in the chain on his ankle. Panting, hair dishevelled, he straightened up. His hands were cuffed tightly behind his back.

The taller woman paced back down the room. She seated herself on the wooden chair. Her wolf mask moved in the direction of the woman with the camcorder. 'I lied,' she said. 'I don't think we should let him go.'

The second woman's voice was softer now. 'I'd let him go.'

'You would?'

'I'd let him go if he told us what he came here to do. In detail. Don't you think?'

'Oh, maybe if he did that.' Both wolf masks turned to face him. Behind the latex, eyes glinted in shadow. Painted white teeth gleamed. 'Maybe.'

He froze, thinking, If I keep very, very still, I may be all right. And if this is what it takes to get me out . . .

He cleared his throat. In a strangled voice, he muttered, 'Water sports. I came for water sports.'

The other woman got up from the chair. She moved back towards the far wall, towards a curtain. Appalled, he thought, She's going to open a *window*? Before he could speak, she thrust the curtain back.

It was not a window. The curtain concealed a full length mirror.

Ben Bright stared into it. The same bare attic room was reflected, lit by the brilliance of the electric bulb.

The difference was that now he could see the white-suited, tethered figure in the centre of the room. He looked from chained ankle to the arms that he could not bring out from behind his back. He looked up, into his own wide, scared gaze. A man in his late twenties, sharp-suited, smart, with every quality accessory. Chained to a wooden beam like a dog.

'Water sports? You'll have to be more explicit,' the wolf with the camcorder said.

Ben couldn't take his eyes off the man in the mirror. He was standing with such a tense stillness, every muscle locked in place. Now he coloured a bright, ashamed crimson, his fair skin flaring from neck to hairline. 'Let me go!'

'What did you come here for?'

'If I say, will you let me go?' he pleaded.

'Of course.' The seated wolf-woman was businesslike. 'Say we're having our first interview. You're here to tell me what you like. Tell me.'

He bowed his head. 'I . . . like to be pissed on.'

'And?'

'And I like . . . to be trained.' Now he could not look his reflection in the eye. 'To piss in my pants and be spanked.'

The room was quiet except for the camcorder's hum.

'Now will you let me go?' he said. He locked his thigh muscles, his buttocks, anything to ease the pressure of his bladder. One of the women laughed. He looked up.

'You're going to piss in your pants,' the taller woman said. 'But first you're going to ask permission. You don't want to know what happens if you do it without permission.'

'But I have to go!' He could see his own wild face in the mirror. Under the urgent desire to urinate, another arousal pushed at his consciousness. The traitor part of his mind said, They do it so well. You might never get another chance like this.

He tugged at his wrists. Immobile. He stared at the mirror. In a slow, cracked voice, he said, 'Please . . . may I piss?'

'Not enough.'

He swallowed, trying to make his mouth less dry. 'Turn the camera off.'

'No.'

Desperation cracked his voice. 'Please . . . may I piss in my pants?'

His crotch tingled. Without warning, and without volition, he let a small stream of piss dribble from his cock. In the mirror, the chained young man stared down. A small dark patch seeped through the crotch of his trousers.

'Oh dear,' cooed the tall masked woman. 'Oh dear . . .'

'I can't hold it!' he groaned. With that he let go and pissed. A heavy warm stream gushed down his thighs. He saw in the mirror the thick golden stream running out of the leg of his trousers. A vast wet patch soaked the crotch and thighs of his pale suit. He squeezed his eyes shut. Acrid hot piss streamed down his legs for what seemed like minutes.

At last the flow eased.

He shifted carefully from one foot to the other. His eyes were still closed tight. Both his socks squelched in his shoes. The wet cloth of his trousers cooled rapidly. Cold wet cloth slid across his crotch as he moved.

His cock twitched, and stiffened.

Shame heated his face. I can't! he thought. This can't be happening to me!

He opened his eyes. He saw in the mirror what the masked woman must be recording with the camcorder. A young man standing with his hands behind his back, the fly and crotch and legs of his suit soaking wet, and the start of an erection poking out the sopping material.

'Oh, dear God,' he said wretchedly.

The taller wolf-woman said, 'He was being truthful. He does like it.'

'Please,' he said miserably, 'I'll do whatever you want, just give me that film, you can do what you like to me, just, please, don't—'

He stopped begging. His cock was getting harder with every word. He shifted damply from foot to foot, staring around, pretending that he was not here, that this was not happening to him.

It didn't work.

I'm on the roller-coaster now, he thought. Childhood memories became stronger. He had pissed his first long trousers on the roller-coaster at the fair, and his mother had raged coldly at him, and nanny had been ordered to lead him back to the car. Through the crowds. With his wet crotch clearly visible to everybody. It would teach him (she said icily) not to do it again.

Ben opened his eyes. He dismissed the camera with a kind of reckless mental shrug: it's done now. They already have enough for blackmail.

I might as well enjoy the rest.

'I wet my pants,' he whined. He noted the two of them glance at each other again. An air of relaxation came over both. The one with the camcorder circled. 'I wet my pants when you said I shouldn't.'

'Then you're a bad boy,' the tall woman said.

A delicious feeling twisted his stomach. His cock hardened in his wet trousers.

'First,' she ordered, 'you can sit in it.'

'But, please—'

'Little boys must be taught!' She walked around

behind him. A few seconds later he felt the right handcuff snap open, and then the left. The cuff on his ankle loosened.

He stood with his arms loose by his sides for a moment. Then, he sank slowly to his knees, and sat down on the urine-wet floorboards. The wood pressed the wet cloth of his trousers up into his crotch. He squirmed.

'I sat in my piss. I sat in my wet pants,' he said. 'Mummy, what do I do now?'

The taller wolf-woman sat on the wooden chair. 'Come and stand here in front of me.'

He walked across the room, stiff-legged. The delicious shame coloured his cheeks. He wanted to wallow in it, rejoice in the freedom.

'Now bend over.'

He felt tears begin to run down his cheeks. Snot leaked out of his nose. He didn't wipe it away. 'No, Mummy, please.'

'You're standing there with your pants soaking wet. Look at that.' She slapped his crotch. His rigid cock throbbed. He bit his lip, almost coming. 'Call that tiny thing a dick? You're a very bad little boy. You have to be punished.'

'Don't hit me, Mummy, please don't.' He snivelled in joyous abandon.

He felt her grab his wrist and pull him down. Her grip shifted to the back of his belt. He fell forward across her lap. There was a short hiatus. He cringed in anticipation.

Her palm caught him hard and squarely across the buttocks. Once, twice, three times.

Helplessly, joyously, sprawled across her, knowing the camcorder must be recording every detail of his humiliation, he came in his pants.

When his last jerking spasms subsided, he fell to the

floor. His come cooled on his limp cock, in his ruined suit trousers. His heaving chest subsided. Airless heat made sweat run down his shaven cheeks, mingling with dust, so that when he rubbed his suit sleeve across his face it came away filthy.

He lifted his head just far enough that he could reach over and kiss the toe of the taller woman's shoe.

She reached up and pulled off the latex werewolf mask.

Black, sweaty hair stuck out from her head. White powder dusted it. Her cheeks, with a similar white film of talcum powder from the mask over them, were nonetheless pink with heat. Her eyes shone and danced. Her mouth curved in a wide, wicked, brattish grin.

'Oh my God.' All the breath went out of his lungs. For one moment he fell back on the floorboards, perfectly still. The cream-coloured Armani suit clung wetly to his crotch and legs.

'Omigod . . .' Ben clamped his arms over his head.

He was not aware he had curled up into a tight foetal ball until he felt a hand – her hand – pulling at his shoulder.

He pushed his head further into the darkness of his body and whimpered.

'Ben!'

'I don't believe it.' Tears ran down his cheeks. He uncurled slightly. A wave of heat went from his head to his toes.

With a pathetic attempt at dignity, he got up. He stood in the bare attic room. He tugged helplessly at one creased cuff. His dick remained completely limp: his humiliation too deep even for arousal. He couldn't look at his ex-wife.

When she spoke, her voice was oddly soft. 'Hello, Ben.'

He yelled, in anguish, 'How could you do this to me!'

'You're going to tell me you didn't like it?'

'Of *course* I didn't like it! All right – I did. But I didn't know it was you!'

She chuckled. When he raised his head, her smile was rueful.

'You can have a copy of the tape as a souvenir, if you like.'

'What do you want, Corey?' He blushed. 'I admit the settlement after the divorce was shabby. That wasn't entirely up to me, you know. I didn't think you'd stoop to blackmail.'

'I don't want money.' Her voice chilled. Then she relaxed, and he remembered, looking at her clear-skinned face, that she could not be any older than twenty-two, even now; hardly older than that day in the registry office when she was eighteen.

He made to step closer. The slimy material of his suit trousers slid up into his crotch.

'Let me go and change,' he pleaded. 'What do you want, Corey?'

'Nothing.' Her voice became hard. 'I get along fine without you in my life. I would get along even better if your mother kept her nose out of my life. I think you ought to suggest she doesn't call me, or come round here, Ben. I think you ought to suggest that very strongly indeed. OK?'

A few hours afterwards, Nadia closed the shop and went back over to Corey's flat. Shannon met her outside and they went in.

'Edited highlights,' Corey said as she put an unlabelled video cassette down on the table. 'There's about ten minutes of really juicy stuff.'

'Edited?' Shannon queried. She flexed her fingers, cramped from holding the camcorder.

'Oh, well . . .' The younger woman looked curiously shame-faced. 'I blacked his head out, OK?'

Nadia raised one dark red eyebrow.

'Ben won't be giving me any more hassle. I guess I think he's suffered enough.' The young woman's expression hardened. 'This one isn't for Ben. It's for Patricia.'

The three women looked at each other.

Shannon said, 'You're right, this one's better for our purposes. Nadia – over to you.'

'Hello? Is that the Conway Hall? I wonder if you can help me. I understand a Mrs Patricia Bright is giving a talk – to the women's charity groups, yes, that's right. A video presentation. Could you tell me when that is, please? The twenty-fourth. That's this Wednesday, isn't it? At seven-thirty. Thank you very much indeed.'

Nadia Kay crossed Red Lion Square in the evening sunlight and made her way to the entrance of the Conway Hall. She wore a light cotton dress in a Laura Ashley print, and flat sandals, and carried a green clutch bag; her make-up was elegant and discreet.

The woman at the door of the main hall smiled automatically but didn't give her a second look.

Nadia kept the smile off her face. The wooden chairs were filling rapidly. Patricia Bright and two other women were up on the stage. The sounds of a low-key altercation about the portable widescreen colour monitor's position drifted down into the audience.

Nadia, looking blamelessly middle-class, and well as though she might be a patron of a charity group, walked down to the front, and along the back of a row of chairs, and past the video tapedeck on the side of the stage.

She didn't look around. She took the videotape in its

cardboard box off the chair it waited on, and put it into her clutch-bag, and set her own equally anonymous tape down in its place. She took a seat five chairs away down the row. No one spoke to her. No one looked in her direction.

The clock ticked towards seven-thirty.

A woman in a pale pink cardigan came and poked at the innards of the video machine and walked away again. She came back with a brown-haired younger woman. They both peered at the machine. One reached down and popped the tape in. The slot whirred and swallowed it. The younger woman nodded. They both walked away.

Seven-thirty. The hall doors closed. Nadia counted, roughly. Between a hundred and a hundred and twenty middle-class women, most of them slightly better dressed than Patricia Bright.

Nadia sat through the interminable introduction, and Patricia's opening remarks about the worthy poor of Mexico City, without even trying to force herself to listen.

The lights dimmed.

'And now,' Patricia Bright said, 'my little video show.'

'I timed it by the hall clock,' Nadia reported back, hardly able to stand up in the telephone booth. 'Absolute *panic*. She couldn't find the remote to turn it off – or even turn it down. *Nine minutes!*'

Chapter Twelve

THEY MET UP with Nadia Kay in the little upmarket pub at the back of the Conway Hall, rushing in, finding themselves among a crowd of extremely well-dressed women whose conversation (Shannon listened as they pushed towards the bar) revolved in hushed and shocked tones around an 'incident' earlier in the evening.

Shannon rubbed her hand under the bridge of her nose and sniffed, hard. She just managed to keep from laughing.

Nadia signalled from a table at the back of the bar. She was halfway through a slim black cigarette and a brandy. A sheen of sweat covered her forehead. She laughed as Shannon pulled up a plush stool. She reached up to grasp Corey's hand.

'Sweetie, never get me doing anything like that again! I thought I'd wet myself. Oh, but you should have seen their faces!'

'I should have seen Patricia's face,' the young woman commented, fetching a five-pound note out of her leather jacket pocket. 'I wish she *did* know it was me! Right: who wants what?'

With Corey at the bar, Shannon leaned back in her

wooden chair and concentrated on listening to Patricia Bright's ex-audience. 'How shockingly *unfortunate*,' she murmured, quoting several of the women. 'Nadia, didn't anyone say anything – stop you – see you?'

The red-haired woman shook her head. Her short bob flew. She stroked strands of hair out of the corners of her eyes. 'No. No! It was unbelievable. I suppose people don't notice, that's the truth of it. They don't see anything they don't expect to see.' She threw her head back and laughed. 'It was beautiful. *I* wish Corey could have seen it.'

The young woman put three glasses neatly on to the table in front of them. 'She's off my back, that's what matters.'

'I don't think you'll hear a whole lot from Ben, either,' Shannon said demurely. 'I do have *some* good ideas.'

The younger woman grinned, sliding her leather jacket off and hanging it on the back of her chair. The pub's doors were open behind her, letting late evening heat drift in.

'Men!' Nadia said.

A few minutes of peaceful silence ensued. Shannon sipped her wine and soda, and began to feel pleasantly buzzed. The pub noise sounded over her head. Music began to beat from the sound system.

'I've got a dare,' Corey Black said suddenly.

Shannon sat up. She looked at the younger woman, startled.

Corey looked at Nadia.

'I dare *you*,' she said, 'to get your own back on that guy.'

Nadia flushed. 'Which "guy"?'

'Oh, yeah, right. The one you've been whining about ever since you got back from Wiltshire! What do you think, Shannon? Is it a good dare?'

Shannon began to grin.

'We dare you,' she said.

But I don't exactly want to 'get my own back', Nadia thought. I just want to prove a point.

Saturday morning. She drove back early from her father's house in Orpington. She was driving towards rain. Ahead, the sky glowed purple. The sun still shone back brightly from the brick and white plaster walls of houses. Then heavy summer rain-drops began to bounce off the gleaming red bonnet of the MG.

She wound the window up most of the way. Traffic held her up in Brixton. She watched people in light summer clothes crowd into shop doorways. A pair of young black women giggled, holding up plastic carrier bags over their hair, and one of them waved at the sports car and blew Nadia a kiss. She returned it, smiling.

By the time she got to Putney Bridge, buildings gleamed under a clearing sky. Patches of blue showed above the City. She drove towards her flat.

She played her messages when she got in.

Oscar's voice on the answerphone was peevish. '*I do think you might have stayed for my speech last week, Nadia. I know I'm no longer your husband, but it looked bad. I had a hell of a job explaining it to His Excellency. Oh, Diane's back from California, she sends her regards. Beeep!*

She stretched out a hand to rewind the machine. It beeped again.

'*Sorry, forgot. That customs chap you want to ask about importing antiques from America, his name is Steven Anson. I've got his address here somewhere, hang on—*'

Nadia copied it down on to the phone pad. She smiled as the answer phone beeped and fell silent. Poor Oscar. He probably *does* think I want Steven Anson's address and number for business purposes.

Little does he know. . .

Nadia's short red hair shone, slightly dishevelled by driving. The morning light emphasised the faint creases at the corners of her eyes. She stroked a finger along silver-framed photos on the sideboard beside her.

Her finger stopped.

The banner in the picture was for a charity she had raised funds for, not long before she and Oscar were divorced.

Good grief. She blinked at the sudden picture that flashed into her mind.

No. I couldn't. It can't be done!

I wonder. Can it?

It would be ideal. . .

Yes!

She dialled. The deep voice that answered the phone made the pit of her stomach leap.

'Steven,' she said. 'Or is it Steve? Yes. It's me. I'll be at your place in twenty minutes. What? Oh – I'm going to show you who's adventurous.' She listened to the phone quack. 'That's all I'm telling you. No. Now. You can go in on shift, or you can phone in sick and come with me. Choose.'

After a moment, she smiled to herself.

'Good. Twenty minutes. Oh, yes. Wear a track-suit.'

'I phoned the long distance weather forecast,' Nadia said as she slowed the MG to a crawl. 'Fortunately, it's going to be fine all day.'

The hot sun gleamed off the MG's red bonnet as she inched it over the speed bump at the gate in the wire perimeter fence. She sneaked a look at Steve Anson.

The big man sat scrunched down in the car. He wore a scruffy but clean white T-shirt, and blue track-suit bottoms and trainers. His heavily muscled arms glimmered with a faint down that thickened to wiry hairs at his wrists, trapped under his thick watch strap.

'This,' he said. 'Is this where you're bringing me?'

Vast expanses of level green grass stretched out to either side of the single-track tarmac road. With the car going slowly now, there was the hot silence that Nadia had always associated with airfields. Leavesdon Airfield, almost in the middle of Watford, might have been in the middle of Dartmoor for all the human activity visible.

'Look,' she pointed. Over to their right, the bubble-globe of a trainer helicopter gleamed in the noon sun, dipping with great care for a practice-landing. She noted a couple of light planes, Cessnas, waiting to go out. She pulled the sports car off into the car park, on the far side of a thin screen of bushes. Beyond them she could see the single-storey buildings and workshops, and the taller flight tower.

'You're *joking*.' He looked around and down at her. 'You think we're going to do it in a *plane*?'

'No.' Nadia left it at that. She swung her legs out, got up from the car, and shut its door behind her. She was wearing an olive green tracksuit, and very small gold studs in her ears. The wind that always blows across airfields brought the scent of flowers, and aviation fuel, and whipped her red hair forward across her eyes.

'I still know one of the instructors here,' she remarked. Then, leaning one hand on the MG for support, she whooped.

'What's so funny?' the big man demanded.

'Nothing.' She looked up as he came around the car and stood beside her. His thick body smelled slightly of cologne, more of sweat. She rested her hands on his flat stomach, slid them up the T-shirt to his hairy pectorals. 'You look so . . . puzzled.'

'Umm.'

Her hands slid lower, across the sun-warmed cloth of his shirt, down to the waistband of his tracksuit. She glanced around, then slid her hand quickly down inside and squeezed his cock. She took her hand out again and inhaled his male scent from her palm. Her flesh swelled and hardened between her legs, and she grew slick.

He put a large hand each side of her head. His rough palms drew her to him, and he touched her lips lightly with his. She inhaled his sweet breath. His lips came down hard. She sucked and bit at his lower lip, tasting him, her body pressed up against him, feeling his hard-on press against her belly through the soft cloth.

'Do you think,' he said raggedly, 'there's anything you'll do that I won't?'

'We'll soon see.' Nadia squeezed his balls lightly through the cloth. 'Better pace yourself, sweets. You have about two hours training to get through first.'

'Training?' he exclaimed loudly. '*Training?*'

'Yeah.' Steve Anson gazed up at the ninety-foot-tall scaffolding tower. 'Right . . .'

'It's no different from jumping off on to the mat,' Nadia grinned. 'Is it, Frank?'

The bearded instructor chuckled. 'About eighty-six feet different, but it's still the same roll. Remember how you've been taught to fall. The rope and harness simulate the static line jump. That's what you'll be doing later.'

'You go first,' Nadia beamed up at the big man generously. 'I'll watch. I've done this before.'

Once, she added mentally. Now I remember that I don't really *like* heights . . . Whatever possessed me to do this before? There must have been easier ways to raise money than a charity parachute jump.

Steve Anson grunted. She watched him follow the

bearded instructor to the foot of the tower. They both began to climb the steel ladder. It seemed long minutes before they reached the top. There was some delay – you don't realise from down here, she remembered suddenly, that at the top it *shifts* in the wind. Then she saw Steve begin to winch up the rope from the last jump, and saw Frank attach it to his body harness. A rope with enough drag on it to simulate an open parachute.

The sweet, hot air caressed her arms. She spread her track-suit top on the grass and sat down. It will be colder on top of the jump tower. It will be colder in the air.

She deliberately didn't look.

'Hey!' Steve Anson sat down heavily beside her on the grass, some minutes later. 'Just like jumping off on to the gym mat!'

His thick brown hair was windswept, and the sun glinted in its first traces of silver at the temples. His face creased into a big grin. He smelled of exertion now, that male smell that made Nadia want to lean forward and bury her face in his crotch.

'Come on, Miss Kay.' Frank might have been smiling under his beard. 'You don't seem to have forgotten anything. It must be, what, two years? Let's see what you make of the tower.'

Climbing the ladder, she momentarily forgot Steve Anson. She stared down at the mat, below, and thought: Remember how to tuck and roll and fall. I can do this. I have done this. Marcia did it and she's ten years older than I am. Remember to keep my eyes open . . .

'Frank!' She shouted over the wind noise at the top of the tower. 'Can we go up today?'

He squinted at the sky. 'Mmm. About three, I'd say.'

*

The flat-roofed, single-storey building looked as though it had been there since World War II. Nadia entered, avoiding the offices, and made her way down to the canteen. The brick walls were painted white. It had windows in each wall. It was bright, and clean, and it smelled of coffee.

She got sandwiches, and fell into conversation with some of the others there: mostly young men and women, and a couple in their fifties. Steve Anson joined her, seating himself carefully on the wooden straight-backed chair.

'Your mate Frank,' he said, when the conversation drifted away from them – two of the younger women were talking about night-flying in rotary wing aircraft.

'Mmm?'

'He's barking mad, isn't he?'

'No more than anyone who flies.' Nadia smiled. 'There's a certain look in the eye. I've noticed it before. They've all got it. They're extremely careful and responsible people. It's just what they *do*.'

His thigh pressed against hers under the table. 'They're not the only ones with that look,' he rumbled. 'Have you seen yourself in the mirror? Woman, you're mad.'

'Not mad,' Nadia said, 'just mildly annoyed.'

'So you want to test my bottle by seeing if I'll jump out of a plane?'

She muttered tartly, 'Consider yourself lucky I've arranged a parachute.'

Steve threw his head back and guffawed, loudly enough to stop all conversation for a second. She couldn't help grinning. She eased back in her chair, a little bruised and jolted by the training jumps, but relaxed. Her body was at ease with itself, her muscles warmed up; just enough anticipatory nervousness to keep her alert.

'Steve.' She touched his arm.

He had rested his elbows on the formica-topped table. Now he looked at her over the rim of his coffee mug. A dab of milk froth decorated his nose. He grinned. 'What?'

'It isn't whether you'll jump out of a plane or not,' Nadia said. 'That's not what I'm interested in. I've had a word with Frank. I think I've talked him into letting me go ahead with this.'

She slid her hand over Steve's warm thigh and into his crotch.

'Tell me,' she said, 'have you ever heard of a tandem jump?'

'You're mad!'

'Completely,' she agreed.

They stood out on the edge of the paved area around the buildings, looking across the airfield runways. Green grass stretched off into the distance. The wind had eased. Somewhere a bird sang.

'A tandem jump is done in a double harness.' She eased her bare arms closer to him, where he leaned on the top bar of the wooden gate. 'Often it's instructor and pupil. It's also a good way for a disabled person to be able to parachute jump. I think I've persuaded Frank we're safe to go tandem.'

Steve Anson gave her a look that was plain bewilderment. 'But . . .'

With confidence and control, Nadia said, 'You jump at ten thousand feet. Static line, square parachute. You have thirty seconds of free-fall. Then there'll be between eight and ten minutes before we have to worry about landing.'

Nadia smiled to herself.

'Track-suits,' she added, 'have no time-consuming belts and zips. You can just pull them down.'

'You *are* mad.'

Around her, now, the air was perfectly still. A hot, windless summer day. Her shadow pooled on the tarmac at her feet. The *whuck-whuck* of a helicopter's rotors sounded from the far side of a hanger. She was silent until it had taken off, the noise thudding away into the distance.

'You don't *have* to do it,' Nadia said.

Nadia slowly pulled on her thin leather gloves.

The aircraft thrummed under her. She sat on the metal-frame set, stomach churning.

'You don't want to skin your hands!' Frank shouted over the engine noise. 'Friction burns can be painful! I'll put you into the harness when we reach ten thousand feet, OK?'

Nadia nodded her head firmly. The air in the body of the plane was chill, through track-suit top and bottom, even with a thick jumper on underneath. The noise was so loud that she could hardly hear herself speak. She sat watching while the bearded instructor put Steve Anson into the double harness: thick nylon straps that encircled his body, came up over his shoulders, around both thighs, and locked centrally at the chest.

'OK?' Frank bawled.

The big man stuck up his thumb.

Using the struts as hand-holds, Frank swung himself forward to the cabin. Nadia saw him leaning over the pilot's shoulder. He tapped the younger man, who half glanced up and slipped one ear-phone off.

Past their heads, through the canopy, she saw a vast sky.

Sharp-edged and perfectly clear, green trees clung to a curved horizon a very long way below. No signs of London. Flying west. And yes, roads down there among the green: one six-lane motorway, a power station on the horizon . . .

A hand grabbed her knee. She jumped.

Steve Anson stroked her cheek. He pointed at the plane's floor, vibrating ten thousand feet above the earth, and his eyebrows went up.

Nadia leaned over and put her mouth to his ear. His flesh was warm under her lips.

'We'll only have five or six minutes to actually do it,' she said. 'Are you up to it?' And she smiled, wickedly.

His lips brushed at her ear. 'You're asking a lot!'

'Perhaps I'd better help you. After all, there won't be any time to spare. You need to be – er – ready to go.' Nadia scrunched up close to him on the wood-covered metal seat. He had put borrowed Doc Martin ankle boots on, and thick leather gloves, and a borrowed thermal track-suit top. Through the cloth, his body had a solid warmth that stirred her groin.

With her eyes on Frank, now leaning on the back of the pilot's seat and looking forward, Nadia spoke into Steve Anson's ear.

'I'd like to have you right here in the plane,' she whispered. 'I'd like to put you down on the floor, and pull your track-suit pants down, and just mount you.'

'Tell me what you'll do.' His breath moistened her cheek. His arm rested down across her back, pressing her into his body.

'I'd stroke your cock, every inch of it. I'd put my hand round, and pull the skin up over your knob, and pull it down; quicker and quicker and quicker. Then I'd straddle you, and push myself down on to you, all hot and wet and swollen with wanting you.'

His breath came raggedly. 'Jesus! Ease up.'

'I'd put my hands under your bum and pull you up inside me. Then I'd gently, gently squeeze.' She stopped, swallowed with a dry mouth. 'I'd put your hands on my breasts. I'd bite your shoulders. I'd feel you thick and hot inside my . . .

He shifted on the seat, and wiped his hand across his face. 'Oh yeah. I'm ready, all right. Come over here, woman – I've got something for you to sit on!'

'Not right now . . .' Nadia laughed. She looked forward. The plane was still climbing. She sat closer to Steve Anson and the parachute pack fastened to his back, all of them crammed on to a narrow vibrating seat. She squirmed, shifting her pussy on the hard surface.

'We both face forward in the harness,' she said. 'I want to be fucked doggy-style. I'm ready.'

'What if someone sees?'

Nadia gave him a challenging smile. 'What if they do?'

'Okay, people.' The bearded instructor walked back from the front of the plane. 'Time to go.'

Frank's hands buckled the straps of the dual harness around Nadia's body, shoulders and thighs. 'We're at ten thousand feet,' he bawled over the noise. 'Call it a thousand feet a minute, you'll have eight or nine minutes to sight-see. Then think about landing! Remember what you know; you'll be fine. OK?'

'Fine!' Nadia shouted. She forced herself not to react to his touch. With difficulty, crab-like, she moved across the plane, Steve Anson's body pressing into her back. His hard-on jutted into her spine. She shifted her body, bringing her buttocks up so that the soft flesh slid across the front of his track-suit.

Frank attached the static line and slid the panel back. A rush of wind sucked at her body. She gasped. Empty air gaped beyond.

'Ready?' Frank bawled.

Nadia heard Steve shout a reply. She nodded, and, as she had done on the previous occasion, very firmly shut her eyes. She walked forward. Someone slapped her shoulder.

The world tripped out from under her feet.

Her stomach clenched. Both her knees came up to her chest and her arms clamped around them. *Wrong,* a voice in her memory said. A great tug and jerk upwards knocked the breath out of her. Steve Anson's body thumped into her back. She spread her arms, and let her legs relax. Her stomach tumbled, turned. She opened her eyes.

'Wheeee!'

The weightlessness resolved itself into falling. Face-down, arms and legs spread wide on the cushioning air. A cold wind rushed at her face. The sky above was a great glass dome, full of light. The circle of the earth was brown, green, grey at the horizon.

'I'm floating!' she yelled, not caring that she couldn't be heard. She looked over her shoulder. The ribbed crimson canopy of the parachute swung above her head, huge at the end of its tethering cords.

Wisps of dark hair whipped at her face. She could not turn her head far enough to see Steve Anson's expression. His body pressed the length of her back. She felt him pull cords, aligning them with landmarks. That little tiny patch of green is an *airfield?* she thought. Oh yes, I remember this . . .

Air rushed past her nostrils, robbing her of breath. The excitement was a swelling rush through her veins. She reached behind herself with a gloved hand and encountered Steve's torso. She pushed her hand between their bodies and cupped her hand over his crotch. His cock was limp.

You just can't rely on some people, Nadia thought dreamily. She began to chafe his flesh through the cloth. The great arc of the sky wheeled about her. That she should be here, now, doing this, fizzed through her body like an aphrodisiac.

She hooked one of her feet up over his ankle, pulling Steve closer down on top of her. With her free hand she reached up under her harness and yanked her track-suit top up. Cold air chilled her stomach and breasts. Her nipples hardened instantly in her lacy bra cups.

Steve's right hand came down and grabbed her breast. They swung wildly in the air. His cock twitched under her hand. She smiled. It swelled until it filled her palm. She pulled her hand away, and stretched out her arms to balance them both in the air.

'Fuck me!' she screamed. Wind whipped her words away.

Blunt fingers probed at her bra. Suddenly both cups were pushed up. Her breasts slipped free. His big hands gripped them. He squeezed, hard. Cold wind and hot flesh covered her. Pleasure stabbed from her nipples to her groin. She felt herself swell, widen, grow instantly wet.

The green was marked now. Hedges demarcated fields, roads snaked across low hills. A line of tiny sparks: reflections from the windscreens of cars, so far below.

I wonder if anyone down there has a pair of binoculars?

Both his hands left her breasts. She gasped, arms still outstretched. The shadow of the canopy whirled across her. His hands slid down her ribs, down to her waist. Fingers hooked under the waistband of her tracksuit bottoms and tugged. The elasticated material slid back. With one heave, he pulled her tracksuit bottoms and knickers together down to her calves.

His legs hooked around her knees.

Cold wind froze her front from neck to crotch. Hot flesh heated her back. His hands gripped her by the hips. She strained to spread her legs, almost pushing their bodies apart. The head of his big cock pushed between her thighs. She threw her head back and yelled into the wind, knowing she could not be heard.

His cock thudded against her labia. Both his hands closed over her breasts, and her erect nipples. The head of his cock pushed between her outer lips. Her flesh widened instantly. His hips thrust. The full thickness of his cock slid up into her cleft. Her sex ran wet, hot. Shudders of pleasure chased all over her skin. She reached out with her arms as if she could hold all the sky.

For a full thirty seconds they fell, his cock thrust into her, her flesh clamped down on his erect flesh, joined in mid-air. He wrapped his arms tightly around her bare ribs. Her bra and track-suit top rucked up under her arms. Her track-suit trousers, around her knees prevented her from widening her legs. She bent her knees very slightly.

She felt his chest heave. He thrust. The wideness of him filled her deliciously, thickly. His sweat-slick flesh chafed her thighs and buttocks. He drove himself up into her, hard. Fire focussed between her legs. She tilted her hips. He drove into her doggy-fashion. His hands and arms clamped their bodies together. A cry swelled in her throat.

The world spun. The disc of the earth whirled underneath her falling body. Sun dazzled her eyes. There was nothing but the big cock slamming up between her legs, the balls banging her belly, the hot thickness of him. His pumping picked up speed. Her neck arched.

The houses and school below seemed exactly the size of children's toys. Toy cars drove along the motorway. Toy trees cast summer afternoon shade on thickly-grassed fields.

Oh *shit!* she thought. This is the height we have to think about landing! Look for landmarks! Prepare – *oh!*

One of his hands grabbed both her breasts in front of her body. His strong fingers dug into her flesh. His other hand, palm flat, pressed her mound up towards him. His hot, naked hips and thighs slammed into her buttocks and the backs of her legs. She hung in the air, their legs intertwined, impaled on his thick cock. Pleasure began to sear up between her legs. Her flesh trembled, spasmed.

Steve Anson came. The feel of his hot come spurting up into her was too much. She flung her head back, body loose in the parachute harness, oblivious of the rushing ground. Her sex convulsed and she thunderously came.

'Quick!' she yelled, as her vision cleared. He could not hear her: she hammered at his body with her fist. The landscape – grass, roads, buildings: the *airfield* – spun and whirled. She felt the cords bite. The canopy's shadow fell across her face. The green grass rushed up.

Bodies together, with total precision, they touched down softly enough to make the tuck-and-roll fall all but unnecessary.

Nadia hit the release catch on the harness.

She lay on her back on the green grass, staring upwards. The blue and sunlit crystal of the sky shone, powerless now that she had firm earth under her again. She began to laugh. She lay half naked, her body hot with satisfaction, with her track-suit rucked up and rolled down, in the corner of the airfield, and she laughed and laughed.

Steve Anson silenced her with a deep kiss.

'Very nice indeed,' she approved. 'My compliments. I shall leave you to deal with the parachute canopy.'

She adjusted her clothes while she watched the big man, bare-arsed, attempt to wind in and control the billowing crimson silk.

Nadia dropped him outside his block of flats.

Steve Anson pushed his fingers through his windswept hair, standing on the pavement by the MG in the evening sun.

'All right,' the big man said. 'All right, I grant you, you got me. That one surprised even me.'

'I thought it might,' Nadia said demurely.

He looked down with dark eyes. 'When do I see you again?'

Nadia shifted the MG into gear.

'When I call you,' she said sweetly. 'If I do . . .'

The three of them met outside the Café Valletta, Monday lunch-time. The leaves of the plane trees were more shabby and dusty in the high summer heat. It took most of the lunch-hour for Nadia to describe her weekend, talking quietly enough not to be overheard by the lunch-time drinkers. Shannon Garrett left her sandwiches untouched. Corey Black drank iced coffee, her heels up on one of the white plastic seats. A stream of black cabs whizzed past the Café Valletta's minute courtyard.

After the congratulations, there was a pause.

'I don't suppose,' Corey said, 'that you have any . . .'

'Photos. Proof. No.' Nadia Kay leaned forward in her chair. She looked at Shannon Garrett. 'As to that – we *still* don't have a winner, do we? But I have an idea.'

Shannon pushed back her brown, curly hair. She said sardonically, 'I generally like your ideas better than I like Corey's.'

Nadia smiled. Her lips had a wicked curve. 'I was thinking, Shannon. You had a good idea yourself, not so long ago. It solved Corey's problem with her flat, and with Ben. And then Corey herself had the idea that I should get my own back on Steven Anson, which was – extremely satisfactory.'

Nadia met Shannon's gaze.

'I have to admit this is partly my idea, and partly Corey's.' She looked at the younger woman, who nodded. Nadia went on, 'Before he leaves for Greece, Shannon – we dare you. Give Tim exactly what he deserves!'

Shannon's eyes lit up.

Her hands clenched into fists.

'Yes,' she said. '*Yes*.'

'Come over to my place tomorrow,' Corey said. She grinned. 'There's a couple of Soho shops I'm going to take Nadia around first. Just for a few bits and pieces . . .'

Chapter Thirteen

THEY GOT BACK to Corey's flat a scant five minutes before Shannon was due.

'I wish you could get all this stuff through catalogues.' Corey held a black PVC bodysuit up against herself. The chains chinked. 'Instead of traipsing halfway across London every time, and having to actually buy it before you know if it suits you. What do you think of this one?'

'Mmm . . . I think it's your size. It doesn't look very durable,' Nadia remarked.

'Well, I'm hardly going to take it back and complain, am I?' The girl tossed the costume back on to the futon. 'You know, I bought this bull-whip once, and by the end of the first weekend afterwards, it *broke*. I tried writing to the credit card company about insurance and they just weren't interested – what's the matter?'

Nadia poised her fingers in front of her curved lips for a moment, and then managed to answer with gravity, 'Nothing. Nothing at all. Are we ready here?'

'I guess so.' The black-haired girl flopped down on the futon. Sunlight shone down from the high windows on to her bare, long legs. She prodded a heap of objects. 'Let's see. Leather mask. PVC bodysuit.

Thigh-boots. Riding crop. Strap-on dildo and harness.'

'Thonged whip,' Nadia said, reaching into the carrier bag beside her chair. She stroked the thin leather thongs between her hands. 'You know, sweets, I just can't understand what men get out of this, myself. Ah well. The enema kit's in the bathroom. Nipple clamps. Cock ring . . . What on earth is *this*?' She held up the last small package she had taken from the shopping bag. It was about eight inches long, and thick enough that she had difficulty closing her hand around it.

Corey reached across and grabbed it. 'That's *lunch*. Chocolate bars, for energy.'

They looked at each other and burst into giggles.

'That has to be all.' Nadia hefted the short-thonged whip. She lifted it and lashed it down on to the futon mattress as the flat's door opened, bringing a breath of summer air. Shannon Garrett walked in.

Nadia beamed at her. 'I think we're more than ready for Tim. It's everything he deserves. Have you worked out how you're going to get him here?'

The curly-haired woman stood in the doorway. She wore a blue cotton print dress and sunglasses. Nadia wished suddenly that she could see her face.

Shannon reached up and took off the sunglasses. Her eyes were red-rimmed.

'I can't go through with it.' Her voice was thick. 'I know you think I'm a mouse, but . . . and I *know* he's a bastard. I just can't help it. I did love him. I'm sorry. I can't do this. And I can't allow you to do it, either.'

A week went past. Then ten days. Shannon's phone stayed silent. Once she caught herself driving past Tim's house on the excuse that he might not have got someone in to feed the two cats. Julia's mother was kneeling on the front lawn, weeding a border. Shannon drove on past, her cheeks hot.

Towards the middle of the month she booked a few days off.

The first morning of her break, she woke and ran herself a deep bath, which she lay in for three-quarters of an hour, reading.

Tim will be back in a fortnight.

She pushed the thought away. She soaped herself, rinsed, and pulled out the plug. A warm breeze drifted in through the bathroom window, raising prickles on her cooling skin. She could smell cut grass from the back garden. She dried herself and sat on the edge of the bath, smoothing body cream into her skin.

I won't see him. I won't phone.

Her cupped palm slid over and around her shoulder, down her arm, stroking across the soft flesh under her bicep. The cream sank into her skin and vanished. She squirted another palmful from the container and smeared it across her breasts. Her hand circled and cupped each slick, heavy breast, smoothing the cream into her skin, and slid down across her stomach to the curve of her belly.

And if he phones me, I won't answer. Or maybe I'll just pick up the phone and tell him that I meant it, I'm not going to be his bit on the side any more.

Her hands slid down her firm thighs, over her knees, down her smooth calves. She stroked cream into her narrow, high-arched feet. Her skin felt warm from the bath, warm from the summer air, clean and refreshed and *handled*.

Maybe I should see him face to face, and tell him. Maybe he'll believe me, this time.

Don't be such a bloody idiot!

If I see him, I'll end up in bed with him; it just seems so natural. And then that's it, I've fucked up.

Come on, Shannon, you told him it was over. Now stick to it!

Shannon belted her long silk robe around her waist and went downstairs. The tiles in the kitchen were cool under her bare feet as she fixed herself cereal, luxuriating in the feeling of being at home, not at work, at eleven o'clock in the morning.

As she went into the living-room, a white envelope caught her eye, on the mat by the front door. She put the cereal down and went to pick it up. The handwriting was familiar.

Nadia? she thought. Oh, fine. What's the matter, you couldn't pick up a telephone and say, Never mind a stupid dare, we're still your friends?

She slit the envelope and took out a sheet of paper.

Sweets, it read.

I've been talking with young Corey, and she and I both think that we need one more dare to decide on the winner of our competition. Therefore, we have both decided to dare you to deal with Tim yourself.

But first – we dare you to go to Gatwick Airport, pick up the first attractive man you see, and fly out with him to wherever he happens to be going!

Corey has transferred some of her 'American' money into your account, for spending. It should cover a standby ticket.

Do you dare?

Don't forget your passport.

Love, Nadia. And, scrawled after, *Do it! Corey. xx.*

Shannon folded the sheet of paper in two and put it into the pocket of her robe. She paced back across the living-room floor, the carpet rough under her bare feet, sat down in the armchair, cradled her bowl of cereal and began to eat.

Nadia. Corey. Don't be so stupid. I don't want dares, I don't want to have sex with another strange man, I just want Tim, and I can't have him!

196

She wiped a tear that slid down the side of her nose with the hand that held her spoon. Milk spattered her robe.

'Oh, shit!' In a temper, she stood up and slammed down the bowl. 'Oh, all right, then! Oh, what the hell – *I'll do it.*'

Shannon Garrett sat in the viewing gallery of the airport bar.

What caught her attention was the prevalence of bags. Suitcases, rucksacks, matched luggage: all the hurrying crowds of people trailing their baggage behind them on wheeled trolleys or trailers. Armed security officers cradled bullpup rifles. She nudged her own overnight shoulder bag with her foot, just to check that it was still there.

'Excuse me, I wonder if you know when the flight for Düsseldorf is leaving?'

Shannon glanced up from her chair. She took in the young, lean, muscled man in blue shirt and casual slacks. He was blond, and he had fair stubble that might pass for a beard in some lights.

'Try looking at the departures board,' she said icily, and turned back to her drink.

She stared down the concourse. Business class, holiday class . . . A throng of people passing rapidly through the terminal, pausing only at the chemists and W H Smiths concession stands; or sitting with differing degrees of anticipation and nervousness in the rows of moulded plastic seating. Outside the plate-glass windows, planes roared down the runway at what seemed like two-minute intervals.

You're the third in half an hour, Shannon thought, sparing a glare for the man's departing back. Give me a *break.*

This was a bad idea. I shouldn't have come. I know

197

Nadia and Corey want me to agree to sort Tim out when he gets back, but I don't want to do that, and I don't want to do this, and what *do* I want to do?

Shannon left her seat, and her untouched drink. She slung her bag over her shoulder and walked down the concourse. Towards the automatic doors that would let her out into the car parks.

Her steps slowed.

I don't know.

She changed direction, moving into one of the seating areas, and put her bag down again. She sat and stared into space.

After some minutes, she became aware that she was staring at the back of a woman wearing a black leather jacket. The woman's hair was black and shiny, and hung in chunky curls. The jacket was a glove-leather version of a biker jacket – Shannon could see the zips up the outside of the forearms, where the woman sat with her arms extended across the backs of the moulded plastic seating. Her shoulders were square. Her lower legs and feet were visible under the seats: she wore sheer black stockings, and ankle boots with a thin, three-inch heel.

Shannon looked away swiftly as the black-haired head began to turn.

I could go back into London. I could go and ask about standby tickets. Maybe I should go on holiday, now I'm here, just a brief break, get away from everything . . .

'Elaine?' a voice said. 'It is Elaine, isn't it? I thought I recognised you.'

Shannon startled and knocked her shoulder bag on to the floor. By the time she picked it up, she could explain her flushed cheeks away as a result of bending over. Small strong hands helped her with the bag.

'Laura,' Shannon said.

The woman's too-wide mouth was sharply defined by crimson lipstick. She had done nothing to the heavy dark line of her brows. The rest of her make-up was either subtle or non-existent, but she had a gloss about her that had not been apparent on the beach.

Shannon held the eye contact. The younger woman met her gaze and did not smile.

Under her biker jacket Laura wore a plain black T-shirt, stretched over her small, full breasts. She was not wearing a bra. Her nipples were two small, hard lumps under the soft cotton.

Shannon let her gaze slide downwards. The woman was wearing a short, tight black leather skirt that barely came down to mid-thigh. The outline of a suspender showed on one thigh, under the leather. Shannon felt her cleft heat, and pulse once.

She squirmed on the plastic moulded seat, staring at the younger woman's ankle boots; anything not to look up and meet those brown-black eyes again.

Then she suddenly, secretly, smiled.

It isn't what they dared me to do. Pretty close, though. I should think it counts . . .

'Actually,' she said, lifting her head, 'it's Shannon. Elaine's my middle name. Shannon Garrett. Have you just flown in?'

The lipsticked mouth opened. Shannon stared at her lips, at her small, square white teeth. She barely registered what the younger woman said.

'Laura Maine. No. I'm flying out to the States at four. I just checked in. I've got a couple of hours to wait.' Still, Laura did not smile, and she held Shannon's gaze. 'Can I buy you a drink?'

Wasn't I supposed to ask you that? Shannon thought wryly. Damn. Oh well. I suppose that means I have to go one better.

'You can buy me a drink,' she said, her belly taut

with anticipation. 'Afterwards.'

The red lips parted. Shannon wanted to reach up and touch their softness with her fingertip. She stayed perfectly still. The other woman slowly nodded.

'Where?' she asked simply.

'I've learned a lot about what I like since I last met you,' Shannon murmured. 'A lot about liking it quick and dirty. A lot about liking it long and slow. A lot about how many different kinds of fucking I like.'

At *fucking*, a slow heat began to rise in the other woman's cheeks. She dropped her eyes briefly. When she looked up, she had begun to smile. 'Buy a ticket. Come to the States with me.'

Shannon stood. She shouldered her bag. She took the younger woman's hand. Laura glanced anxiously around the crowded concourse. She tugged. Shannon tightened her grip.

'What—'

'Next time I'll do what you say,' Shannon whispered, leaning over, her breath feathering the fine hairs of the woman's temple. 'This time you're going to do what I tell you.'

The hand within hers grew warm and still.

Hand in hand, Shannon strode down the concourse. She deliberately walked fast, so that the younger woman had to hurry to keep up. Laura stumbled on her high heels. Shannon grabbed her under the elbow and steered her into the Ladies.

The long tiled and mirrored room was, momentarily, deserted, although some of the cubicles were obviously occupied. Shannon didn't release her grip on Laura's arm. She all but pushed the younger woman into the far-end cubicle. It seemed more spacious than the rest, by virtue of an opaque-glass window.

In a frantic whisper, Laura hissed, 'Just what do you think you're doing?'

Shannon put her hand up. She put four fingers flat on the young woman's mouth, and pushed. The precise red lipstick smeared across her mouth and cheek. Shannon put a hand each side of Laura's head, pulled her forward, and kissed her, thrusting her tongue deep into the woman's mouth, tasting her. The woman whimpered, the stiffness of her body relaxing.

Shannon dropped her hands, pressed them to the woman's body, and slid them up under her arms, under the silk lining of the leather jacket. Zips jangled. she cupped the heavy breasts in her palms.

When their lips parted, Laura said, 'We'll be seen! They'll see more than one person's in here!'

She again pressed her finger to Laura's smeared mouth. Then she put her hands down to the younger woman's waist, and pulled her tight in towards her body. Breasts, bellies, thighs; pressed close together through thin cloth.

Shannon unsnapped the back button of the tight leather skirt. The zip came noisily undone. She felt Laura cringe in her arms. Muffling her face in thick, sweet-smelling curls of black hair, Shannon slid her fingers under the waistband of the woman's skirt and began to ease it down over her round little hips. The pads of her fingers slid over garter belt, suspenders and the cool, naked flesh of the woman's bottom, to the tops of her sheer stockings.

She put her lips on Laura's ear. 'You're not wearing any knickers!'

Shannon's sex grew hotter. She pushed with her thighs, forcing the younger woman back towards the wall. Her calf knocked against the cistern. The black leather skirt slid over Laura's round arse and fell down, hanging up around her knees. For a moment Shannon enjoyed the sight of her: tumbled black curls, smeared lipstick, sweaty skin. The black leather jacket

201

swinging open to disclose short T-shirt, garter belt, black suspenders and stockings, and the curly black tuft of hair at her crotch.

She reached up under the jacket, under Laura's armpits, and hoisted the woman bodily up into the air. Her muscles strained. She stepped forward and sat Laura on the window-ledge. The young woman's body leaped as her nude buttocks came into contact with the cold tiles. She clapped both hands over her mouth. Above them, her wide eyes stared at Shannon somewhere between outrage and arousal, and something that might have been admiration.

Shannon leaned forward. She pushed Laura's thighs apart, easing the woman back against the window. The warm, damp smell of her cleft hit Shannon's nostrils. Breathless, unable to wait, she dipped her head between the woman's cool, suspender-clad thighs. She licked one delicate wet stroke across Laura's clitoris. The body under her hands throbbed.

Her hands bit into Laura's thighs. She felt the woman's small, square hands knot in her hair. She put her mouth down into the woman's sex, burying her face in the hot wet readiness, inhaling the musky woman scent. She let her tongue caress the outer labia; then plunged it hard down into the secret interior. The hands in her hair gripped hard, tugged; she didn't stop. Flickering, first fast, then slow, then relentlessly pushing the woman towards an uncontrollable release, she thrust her tongue deep between Laura's legs. Outside, someone ran a tap into a washbasin. Someone else flushed a cistern, further down the cubicles.

Balanced between the throbbing wetness between her own legs and the delicious likelihood of discovery, Shannon stuck one hand down her own knickers. She rubbed, hard, still thrusting her tongue into the woman's sex. The woman's body jerked. The hands pulled her hair hard. Laura's lithe, muscular thighs suddenly tightened and released. Shannon's own sex exploded. She felt warm wetness slick her whole hand. Laura's hot, sweating body collapsed to lean on top of her, rapid deep breathing stifled.

'You cow!' the young woman whispered. 'I'll pay you back for that! Are you coming to New Orleans with me?'

Despite her flushed, triumphant face, Shannon said coolly, 'I suppose I'd better see about tickets.'

Their seats were not together. At least, Shannon thought, we got on to the same plane.

She sat across the aisle, a few seats back, watching Laura stare out of the window. Her pillar-box red lipstick was again precise. Her leather jacket encased her strong shoulders. She sat with her legs crossed, neat ankle boots just visible from where Shannon was sitting. To anyone else, she seemed a collected, seasoned traveller, perfectly unshaken by take-off or flight. *I* know you're not wearing any knickers, Shannon thought, and felt herself grow hot again between her legs.

She staggered as she stood, stepping into the aisle. The throbbing of the gangway underfoot reminded her they were six miles above the earth's surface. She made her way towards the toilets at the back.

They were mostly unoccupied. She chose one. As she got the door open, a body crashed into her back, pushing her forward into the cubicle. The door slammed shut behind them. Shannon opened her mouth to shout and recognised, in the dim light, Laura's grin. There was not room for two people.

With no preamble, Laura grabbed her and kissed her. Then she put her hands on Shannon's shoulders and turned her around to face the back of the cubicle.

The airframe shook. Shannon glimpsed them both in the mirror. Then a hand took her own left hand, and pulled it down and planted it on the wall at the back of the toilet. Her right hand was similarly pulled down.

Shannon leaned with her weight on her arms, her legs apart, over the empty toilet. She felt Laura's hands stroking her ass. 'What the hell are you doing? They'll throw us off!'

'They won't even notice if you keep quiet.' Laura's eyes gleamed wickedly in the mirror. 'I had to.'

With her head craned, Shannon saw Laura put her handbag down by the sink. The reverberations of flight drummed through her taut, spread legs. Laura opened her handbag. She took out a cream-coloured six-inch vibrator.

'Always such fun to explain to Customs,' she purred. She twisted the end firmly. Shannon heard it buzz even over the flight noise. Her sex grew damp, wet, then soaking in the space of seconds. The tight fabric of her panties rode up into her crotch, irritating her labia.

Laura drew the buzzing vibrator's tip down Shannon's spine, down between her buttocks. It buzzed at the entrance of her anus. Shannon's legs stiffened. She jammed her ass up. The vibrator slid down into the wetness of her sex.

Laura's arm snaked under her body. Her strong hand pulled the front of Shannon's dress down. Shannon felt her breasts squeezed out of her bra cups. They hung free, the skin tingling with sensitivity. The woman's hands stroked her. Fingers circled her nipple. Suddenly they pinched, just hard enough to make Shannon gasp. Her nipples hardened instantly.

The vibrator thrust between her spread legs. She braced herself as it thrust in, prizing her hot flesh apart. The woman's hand, where she held it, thumped into Shannon's crutch with every forward stroke. Her flesh loosened, swelled, streamed with juices. She lifted her hips, her throat stretching as her head arched up and back.

The hand squeezed closed on her breast. The pitiless vibrator was slammed up inside her and kept there, Laura's hand firmly across her fanny. Shannon bit her lip and moaned. Her legs shook. Warm arousal flooded every inch of her skin, then zeroed in on her crutch. She almost screamed with anticipation. Her body peaked. She flooded. Her sex convulsed. The explosion of pleasure knocked her to her knees, sprawled across the open seat of the toilet. Sweat soaked her hair and ran down into her eyes. Every muscle of her body shook with release.

The airplane toilet door clicked closed behind Laura's departing back.

Shannon left it a decent number of minutes before she vacated the cubicle. She tried to tidy herself up. When she walked back down the aisle, her face burned, although no one gave her a second look. The crotch of her knickers was soaking wet.

Laura sat in her seat, gazing out of the window again past her fellow-passengers. She was unchanged but for the tiny smile that remained on her lips for the rest of the flight.

They changed planes at Atlanta. They hardly spoke, neither then nor on the hour-long flight to New Orleans. Travelling into the Big Easy, under an immense blue sky, it was still glorious daylight. Shannon sat thigh to leather-covered thigh with Laura in the taxi. She paid more attention to the feel of that against her sweat-soaked, humid skin than she did to the streets and skyscrapers, and she barely registered the name of the hotel Laura booked them into. She was only aware of the ache in her sex, and her realisation of how much remained untried with this woman's body, this garden of pleasures.

The hotel room was moderately big, with a pair of wide windows that let in the sun. They faced the windowless back wall of a factory, Shannon saw, throwing her overnight bag on to one of the two double beds, and they were on the sixth floor.

A hand slid up between her legs.

Shannon turned around. She reached up and grabbed Laura's shoulders. The black leather was soft and warm under her hands. She pushed the woman back. The edge of the bed caught Laura behind the knees, and she fell backwards with Shannon on top of her.

Pressed warm body to warm body, Shannon found herself running with sweat. She reached up and triggered the air-conditioning, in a desperate attempt to overcome New Orleans' humidity. The material of her summer dress was wet under her arms, across her bust, down her stomach. She lowered her head and put her face into the hot cleft of Laura's breasts. The younger woman struggled to hook her legs around Shannon's hips.

'Oh no,' Shannon said. 'After the plane? I've got a little surprise for you. You may like it. I certainly will . . .'

Without getting off Laura's compact, muscled body, Shannon reached across and tugged the zip of her overnight bag. She fumbled her hand inside, among the change of clothes and bathroom bags.

She brought out her hand, holding the handle of a short-thonged black leather whip.

Laura's eyes brightened. 'No, no,' she whimpered, writhing under Shannon's imprisoning weight. She looked up from under long, long lashes. The lipstick on her wide mouth was mussed again. 'You wouldn't beat me, would you?'

Shannon sat back up, dragging the younger woman across her lap. She lifted the whip, and brought the thongs down on the taut leather stretched across Laura's buttocks. The slap was loud in the room, over the hum of the air-conditioner. Laura yelped.

Shannon raised her arm again. She brought the whip down across the backs of the woman's thighs, in the gap between stocking-tops and skirt. Laura's mound pressed hard down on to her thigh. Her torso shuddered, inhaling a deep, sharp breath. She moaned.

Shannon whipped the thongs down. The flesh of the woman's legs began to glow pink. Her whole body writhed with arousal, under Shannon's imprisoning hand. She wriggled. She pushed her breasts against Shannon's leg. Her tangled black hair flopped down over her face. Shannon brought the whip down with a solid *crack!*

'Please!' the young woman said. 'Fuck me! Fuck me until I can't stand up! Please!'

Shannon reversed the whip in her hand. She thrust the slick, thick leather handle up between Laura's legs. The smooth knob on the end met resistance. Gently, she pushed. The whip handle slid smoothly up into the other woman's sex. Shannon drew it back, thrust it forward, with long, slow strokes. She ground her own sex against the rough cover on the bed, thrusting her wet crutch down with force. As Laura moaned and whimpered, she increased the tempo, thrusting the whip handle with a rapid friction. Laura's head went back and she yelled like a banshee. At the same moment Shannon's sex became too aroused for her to think. She let the young woman fall from her knees on to the floor, and took the handle of the whip, and thrust it up between her own legs. The solid bulk inside her filled her so that she came, and came, and came. She slid down, exhausted, to lie beside Laura.

The younger woman grinned lazily through tangled, sweat-wet hair; reached over, and enfolded Shannon in her warm and welcoming arms.

Chapter Fourteen

SHANNON WOKE TO the fifth day. Not sprawled up against Laura Maine's solid, cat-curled spine, this time, but stretched across warm, empty sheets.

When she could rub the sleep out of her eyes enough to read, the note on the pillow said *Love to do this again sometime*. It added a phone number, then: *P.S. The room is paid up to the end of the week. Enjoy!*

She rolled over and lay on her back for a while. The air-conditioning hummed. Outside, New Orleans gleamed under a blue sky. When she rose, naked, and pushed the window up an inch, she smelled mud, fish, urine, roses, patchouli, fresh bread, seafood cooking, and a dozen other smells she could not name.

I know there's something I was supposed to do.

Oh my God, Tim! I forgot the dare about Tim!

She stretched her naked arms up to the sun and stretched; every muscle in her body relaxed, her sex satisfied and content.

In a foreign country, three thousand miles from home.

I did forget him, didn't I? He never crossed my mind. So much for the dare.

It was not until several hours later, sitting in a coffee

shop in the French Quarter, that Shannon Garrett suddenly laughed out loud. The waitress gave her a startled look.

'I'll have another hazelnut cappuccino,' Shannon said. She beamed and looked out at the narrow, teeming streets.

Of course. It wasn't a dare. It was a present. A present from Nadia and Corey. And it was just what I needed.

Nadia groped for the phone. She switched the bedside lamp on, knocking a 1950s bedside clock to the floor. She groped for it and looked at the face. She recognised the voice on the phone.

'Shannon Garrett, *do you have any idea what time this is?*'

She listened.

'Really? This, may I remind you, isn't New Orleans! This is London. What on earth is so urgent?'

Nadia Kay listened some more.

When she finally put the phone down on the transatlantic call, she flopped back against her pillows. Her window was just growing light with the summer dawn.

She reached for the phone again and dialled.

'Corey, my sweet. Yes. Yes, I *do* know what time it is. I've just had a call from Shannon. She's in New Orleans. Yes. What did she phone for? Oh,' Nadia said, snuggling down, her eyes on the brightening window. 'She says, thanks. She says, her room is paid for, for the week. She says, would we like to come out and join her?

'She says she's got an idea for some *international* dares . . .'

Already published

BACK IN CHARGE
Mariah Greene

A woman in control. Sexy, successful, sure of herself and of what she wants, Andrea King is an ambitious account handler in a top advertising agency. Life seems sweet, as she heads for promotion and enjoys the attentions of her virile young boyfriend.

But strange things are afoot at the agency. A shake-up is ordered, with the key job of Creative Director in the balance. Andrea has her rivals for the post, but when the chance of winning a major new account presents itself, she will go to any lengths to please her client – and herself . . .

0 7515 1276 1

THE DISCIPLINE OF PEARLS
Susan Swann

A mysterious gift, handed to her by a dark and arrogant stranger. Who was he? How did he know so much about her? How did he know her life was crying out for something different? Something . . . exciting, erotic?

The pearl pendant, and the accompanying card bearing an unknown telephone number, propel Marika into a world of uninhibited sexuality, filled with the promise of a desire she had never thought possible. The Discipline of Pearls . . . an exclusive society that speaks to the very core of her sexual being, bringing with it calls to ecstasies she is powerless to ignore, unwilling to resist . . .

0 7515 1277 X

HOTEL APHRODISIA
Dorothy Starr

The luxury hotel of Bouvier Manor nestles near a spring whose mineral water is reputed to have powerful aphrodisiac qualities. Whether this is true of not, Dani Stratton, the hotel's feisty receptionist, finds concentrating on work rather tricky, particularly when the muscularly attractive Mitch is around.

And even as a mysterious consortium threatens to take over the Manor, staff and guests seem quite unable to control their insatiable thirsts . . .

0 7515 1287 7

AROUSING ANNA
Nina Sheridan

Anna had always assumed she was frigid. At least, that's what her husband Paul had always told her – in between telling her to keep still during their weekly fumblings under the covers and playing the field himself during his many business trips.

But one such trip provides the chance that Anna didn't even know she was yearning for. Agreeing to put up a lecturer who is visiting the university where she works, she expects to be host to a dry, elderly academic, and certainly isn't expecting a dashing young Frenchman who immediately speaks to her innermost desires. And, much to her delight and surprise, the vibrant Dominic proves himself able and willing to apply himself to the task of arousing Anna . . .

0 7515 1222 2

THE WOMEN'S CLUB
Vanessa Davies

Sybarites is a health club with a difference. Its owner, Julia Marquis, has introduced a full range of services to guarantee complete satisfaction. For after their saunas and facials the exclusively female members can enjoy an 'intimate' massage from one of the club's expert masseurs.

And now, with the arrival of Grant Delaney, it seems the privileged clientele of the women's club will be getting even better value for their money. This talented masseur can fulfil any woman's erotic dreams.

Except Julia's . . .

0 7515 1343 1

PLAYING THE GAME
Selina Seymour

Kate has had enough. No longer is she prepared to pander to the whims of lovers who don't love her; no longer will she cater for their desires while neglecting her own.

But in reaching this decision Kate makes a startling discovery: the potency of her sexual urge, now given free rein through her willingness to play men at their own game. And it is an urge that doesn't go unnoticed – whether at her chauvinistic City firm, at the château of a new French client, or in performing the duties of a high-class call girl . . .

0 7515 1189 7

A SLAVE TO HIS KISS
Anastasia Dubois

When her twin sister Cassie goes missing in the South of France, Venetia Fellowes knows she must do everything in her power to find her. But in the dusty village of Valazur, where Cassie was last seen, a strange aura of complicity connects those who knew her, heightened by an atmosphere of unrestrained sexuality.

As her fears for Cassie's safety mount, Venetia turns to the one person who might be able to help: the enigmatic Esteban, a study in sexual mystery whose powerful spell demands the ultimate sacrifice . . .

0 7515 1344 X

SATURNALIA
Zara Devereux

Recently widowed, Heather Logan is concerned about her sex-life. Even when married it was plainly unsatisfactory, and now the prospects for sexual fulfilment look decidedly thin.

After consulting a worldly friend, however, Heather takes his advice and checks in to Tostavyn Grange, a private hotel-cum-therapy centre for sexual inhibition. Heather had been warned about their 'unconventional' methods, but after the preliminary session, in which she is brought to a thunderous climax – her first – she is more than willing to complete the course . . .

0 7515 1342 3

SHOPPING AROUND
Mariah Greene

For Karen Taylor, special promotions manager in an upmarket Chelsea department store, choice of product is a luxury she enjoys just as much as her customers.

Richard – virile and vain; Alan – mature and cabinet-minister-sexy; and Maxwell, the androgynous boy supermodel who's fronting her latest campaign. Sooner or later, Karen's going to have to decide between these and others. But when you're shopping around, sampling the goods is half the fun . . .

0 7515 1459 4

Forthcoming publications

INSPIRATION
Stephanie Ash

They were both talented painters, but three years of struggling to make a living from art have taken the edge off Clare's relationship with her boyfriend. The temptation to add a few more colours to her palette seems increasingly attractive – and proves irresistible when she meets the enigmatic and charming Steve.

But their affair is complicated when Steve's beautiful wife asks Clare to paint his portrait as a birthday surprise. Clare is more than happy to suffer for her art – indulging in some passionate studies of her model *and* her client – but when a jealous friend gets involved the situation calls for more intimate inspiration . . .

0 7515 1489 6

DARK SECRET
Marina Anderson

Harriet Radcliffe was bored with her life. At twenty-three, her steady job and safe engagement suddenly seemed very dull. If she was to inject a little excitement into her life, she realised, now was the time to do it.

But the excitement that lay in store was beyond even her wildest ambitions. Answering a job advertisement to assist a world-famous actress, Harriet finds herself plunged into an intense, enclosed world of sexual obsession – playing an unwitting part in a very private drama, but discovering in the process more about her own desires than she had ever dreamed possible . . .

0 7515 1490 X

[ ]	Back in Charge	Mariah Greene	£4.99
[ ]	The Discipline of Pearls	Susan Swann	£4.99
[ ]	Hotel Aphrodisia	Dorothy Starr	£4.99
[ ]	Arousing Anna	Nina Sheridan	£4.99
[ ]	Playing the Game	Selina Seymour	£4.99
[ ]	The Women's Club	Vanessa Davies	£4.99
[ ]	A Slave to His Kiss	Anastasia Dubois	£4.99
[ ]	Saturnalia	Zara Devereux	£4.99
[ ]	Shopping Around	Mariah Greene	£4.99

X Libris offers an eXciting range of quality titles which can be ordered from the following address:

Little, Brown and Company (UK),
P.O. Box 11,
Falmouth,
Cornwall TR10 9EN

Alternatively you may fax your order to the above address.
FAX No. 0326 376423.

Payments can be made as follows: cheque, postal order (payable to Little, Brown and Company) or by credit cards, Visa/Access. Do not send cash or currency. UK customers and B.F.P.O. please allow £1.00 for postage and packing for the first book, plus 50p for the second book, plus 30p for each additional book up to a maximum charge of £3.00 (7 books plus).

Overseas customers including Ireland please allow £2.00 for the first book plus £1.00 for the second book, plus 50p for each additional book.

NAME (Block Letters) _____

_____

ADDRESS _____

_____

_____

☐ I enclose my remittance for _____

☐ I wish to pay by Access/Visa card

Number _____

Card Expiry Date _____